To Chakka,

Walk-Foot Woman
and Other Poems

Words that will live forever now that you've given birth to them. Inspirational words from Chakka.

Walk good,
Dr Kelvin McClymont
26/7/2024

**Other Books by the Author
(aka Kate Elizabeth Ernest)**

A Home for Mr. No-Roach (2024);
Little River (2022);
Tricky Tricky Twins (1997);
Birds in the Wilderness (1995);
Festus and Felix (1994);
Hope Leaves Jamaica (1993).

Walk-Foot Woman and Other Poems

Velma McClymont

WOMANZVUE LTD
61 Bridge Street, Kington, Herefordshire, HD5 3DJ

A WOMANZVUE BOOK

This book was first published in Great Britain in 2024
by WomanzVue Ltd
61 Bridge Street, Kington, Herefordshire, HD5 3DJ

Copyright © Velma McClymont, 2024

Velma McClymont has asserted her right under the Copyright.

Designs and Patents Act 1988 to be identified as the author of this work.

All rights reserved. No part of the publication may be reproduced or transmitted in any form or by any means, electronic or mechanical, including photocopying, recording, or any other information storage or retrieval system, without the permission in writing from the publishers.

A catalogue record for this book is available from the British Library.

ISBN: 978-1-7397247-3-3

Cover design by Rebecca Smith
Typeset in 11 on 13pt Garamond MT Pro
by Paul Medcalf, Avocet Typeset,
Bideford, Devon, EX39 2BP
Printed and bound in Great Britain by CPI Group (UK) Ltd.,
Croydon, CR0 4YY

To find out more about the poet/author and her books, please visit
https://www.womanzvue.com

This book is dedicated to the memory of my beloved grandmother: Mrs Carmel Smith-Morris (1909–2008).

"If a man is not faithful to his own individuality, he cannot be loyal to anything."
– Claude McKay.

"A people without knowledge of their past history, origin and culture is like a tree without roots."
– Marcus Garvey.

CONTENTS

Preface	11
Introduction	13
Foreword	16
PART ONE: WALK-FOOT WOMAN	**19**
Walk-Foot Woman	20
Pilgrim Stick	21
The Change	22
The Mad Doctor of Edinburgh Castle	23
The Island of Springs: Ode to the West Wind	24
Drumilly Remembered	25
Moving Up	26
A Better Future: Ode to Langston Hughes	27
If We Must Live	28
Insurmountable Heights: Ode to Marcus Garvey	29
The Ivory Tower: Ode to The White House	30
The Shadows: Ode to Walter de la Mare	31
Liquid Sunshine	32
Black Forest Gateaux	33
Sea Breeze	35
"Heart of Oak"	37
Eight Rivers	38
Footprints Upon Our Souls	39
Fossils in Rocks	40
David Livingstone's Promised Land	41
Afrikan Remembrance Day	42
Barbed Wire on the Western Front	43
The Call to Action	44
Mutiny in Taranto: Ode to Mr James Fairweather	46
Ration Books in Battersea	48
"No Coloureds, No Irish, No Dogs"	50
No More Dreams to Chase	51
The Kentuckian King of Boxing	52
Brooklyn Heights	54
The Way West	56

Neighbourhood Watch	58
Brexit; Or Peddling Hyperbole	59
Diaspora Daughters of Africa	61
Shoot for the Stars	63
"Blackleg"	65
Word Glut	66
Diversion Tactics	67
One of Us	68
Mistaken Identity	69
Bread Basket: Ode to Maya Angelou	70
The Pearl Necklace: Ode to The Daffodils	71
Air Mail Letters	72
Space Invader: Ode to Star Trek	73
The Reaper's Garden	74
Foodies: Colour Coding	75
Terra Firma	76
The Yellow Butterfly	77
Black Velvet	78
Burning Spear: Ode to Robert Burns	79
The Squatters	80
The Chameleon	81
Housemaid's Knee	82
Dog Roses	83
On the Brink	84
The Fickle Weather	86
Watery Wealth	87
The Water Carrier	88
The Dance of the Snakes	89
The Crossing	90
Selfie With Nye Bevan	91
I Wonder Why: Ode to Jeannie Kirby	92
The Colon-Man: Ode to The Pedlar's Caravan	93
Saturday's Child	94
Jippy-Jappa Hat	95
Fire Sparkle	96
The Hills of Zion: Ode to Charles Kingsley	97
The Collectors of Souls	98
The Flame Tree: Ode to Thomas Hood	99
The Mentor	100

Comfort: On the Death of a Neighbour's Daughter (1982)	101
Comfort: The Vigil	102
Garden Statuary	103
Kerosene Light	104
Celebrity Fridge	105
Voices	106
Taking Words Apart	107
Block Capitals	108
A Garland of Words	109
Some People	110
The Eye of the Egg	111
Gourd Tree: Ode to the Little Nut Tree	112
The Good Samaritan	113
Pink Bus to Battersea (2015)	114
Digging Up the Past: Independence Day	115
Easter Monday	116
Our Coat of Arms	117
Yabba Pot: The Good Old Days	118
Forget-Me-Not	120
Jamaican Talls	121
Compulsive Walkers	122
Black Loyalist Beggars	123
The Archway of No Return	124
The Imperialist Yoke	126
Enemies of the Empire	127
Calico Petticoat Rebellion	128
Merchant City	130
Ode to Joseph Knight and James Somerset	131
Flinging Greek Fire at Meghan Markle	132
The View from Cardiff Castle: For Meghan Markle	134
Whitewashing the Past	135
Indelible Ink: The Triangular Trade	136
Sonnet 18: Trade Winds	137
Hurricane Dean (August 2007)	138
Unchaining the Imagination	139
I Shall Return	140
Black Ivory: Call and Response	141
The Stone-Breakers	142
A Girl Writes Back: Ode to Rudyard Kipling	143

The Stranger in the Room	146
Kool-Aid	147

PART TWO: BRAATA — 149

Meghangate	150
"What Meghan Wants"	151
Waiting to Exhale	152
Scenes From Gatwick Airport	153
Guava Tree Over Cocoon Pond	155
Gaze on a Grecian Goddess	156
Scenes in Papine Market, Kingston (August 1999)	157
Celebrity Spotting at JFK Airport (June 2012)	158
Victory in Sight: For HW Longfellow	159
Mother and Child at Bus Stop	160
Echoes	161
Blue Print: Upon a Father-in-Law's Death	162
Cocoa Basket: Upon a Grandmother's Death (July 2008)	163
Dead Silence: Upon Losing a Child (December 1989)	164
Thread-Bag: Upon Losing a Great-Aunt to Dementia	165
The Drowning: Green Grotto Cave	166
Grumpy Old Man	167
Swan Lake Neck	168

Postscript: Reflections On Walk-Foot Woman and Other Poems	169
Acknowledgements	174
About the Author	175

PREFACE

The Making of Walk-Foot Woman and Other Poems

In 1990, when my daughter (Rebecca) was two-years old, one of my poems was published in a magazine for parents of preschool-age children. Although the publication of a single poem about childhood is a distant memory, it encouraged me to write a collection of poetry on an Amstrad computer. However, it was not until May 2006, when a fifteen-year-old schoolboy named Kiyan Prince was fatally stabbed in London, that I felt moved to write a poem for public performance. Titled "If We Must Live", this emotive poem was also inspired by my muse, the Jamaican-born writer and poet Claude McKay, whose protest poem, "If We Must Die", is globally celebrated.

Over the years, I have recited "If We Must Live" in Jamaica (Ocho Rios High School and St Ann's Bay Library – Marcus Garvey Archive), Scotland (Glasgow Women's Library) and many places in London. In 2012, having spent over three months in New York, I found myself writing on the subway and in two local libraries (Flatlands and New Lots). I have included several poems from my sojourn during that time, including "Brooklyn Heights", which was inspired by a visit to Brooklyn Museum in May 2012. Whilst there, I viewed the feminist exhibition titled *The Dinner Party* by Judy Chicago.

Upon my return to the UK in 2012, I turned my attention to revising my historical novel, *Little River*, which I worked on in New York. During moments of respite from the novel, I felt the need to write what I call "slabs of poetry", especially whilst visiting Scotland between July 2014 and April 2017. Poems such as "Ode to Joseph Knight and James Somerset", "Merchant City", "Burning Spear: Ode to Robert Burns" and "The Stranger in the Room" were written for performance at Glasgow Women's Library during the launch of the Commonwealth Women Writers' Project in November 2014.

Thirty-four-years after my first poem appeared in print, it is my pleasure to share this collection with readers, which includes autobiographical poems about my personal experiences of anti-Black racism at school in London, travels abroad, and in the workplace. It is also worth noting that, over the last few years, I have produced five collections of poetry. *Walk-Foot Woman and Other Poems* is the first to be published. With an emphasis on the spoken word, the book explores a range of subjects: Britain's role in transatlantic slavery, representation, otherness, place/displacement, childhood, journeying, the Windrush generation, race, class, gender, nature, religion and so on.

Born into two cultures in colonial Jamaica – African-Caribbean and British – I have been inspired by poems such as Walter de la Mare's "The Listeners", John Masefield's "The West Wind", William Wordsworth's "Daffodils", Robert Burns' "A Red Red Rose" and Charles Kingsley's "The Sands of Dee" among others. In an act of decolonising the poet's mind, I have drawn on the works of Langston Hughes, "A Dream Deferred", Maya Angelou's "No Loser No Weeper" and Claude McKay's "The White House" to name but a few. The Hon. Louise Bennett's focus on the Jamaican people's mother tongue (*patois*) is captured in "Yabba Pot: The Good Old Days" and haikus such as "Scenes in Papine Market." Influenced by the great Marcus Garvey, "Insurmountable Heights: Ode to Marcus Garvey" speaks for itself.

Dr. Velma McClymont.

INTRODUCTION

Like a slide projector, *Walk-Foot Woman* reels through the many experiences and emotions that have shaped the life of its poet, Velma McClymont, but which will resonate in the hearts and minds of all who read her words. The title is taken from the very first poem, "Walk-Foot Woman," which introduces the reader to the historical and personal memories that resurface across the collection. From the first line, we are transported to a place where past, present and future collapse. The voice of an enslaved ancestor – an earthbound spirit or perhaps a *maroon*[1] – calls out to the walk-foot woman as she moves through a woodland glade in Jamaica. As with many of the poems, English and Jamaican are beautiful worked together. We hear the "smack rather like a *sibble jack*" (a vine once used to beat enslaved Africans) as it lashes out from the bushes. Through this spectral act, we are reminded that Mother Nature is a site of ancestral memory, housing a deep-rooted and unhealed pain that can be unleashed at any moment.

And so, the journey begins, chasing history, memories and the complexities of British Caribbean identity back and forth across the Atlantic, reminding us of the multiple journeys and crossings that can be traced from African civilisations to the transoceanic trafficking and enslavement of African peoples all the way through to the present day. We are both invited to remember the pain of separation from "Mother Africa" whose "Laugh shatters the sorrow" of her "lost child, Kofi" (in "Eight Rivers") and recall that "No public apology or reparations" has yet been made to those who "rocked the colonial cradles" (in "Forget-Me-Not"). At the same time, when memory becomes too painful to revisit, and loss too deep to fathom, we are invited to select only "the memories worth keeping," while shedding "those that hurt us like sticks and stones": "Think only that we loved and we lived well" (in "Footprints Upon Our Souls").

Crossing the Atlantic to the UK, the collection remembers the difficulties and achievements of the Windrush Generation (1948–1971) who helped to rebuild post-War Britain.[2] As a "Windrush

---

1. *Maroons* are Africans who resisted being enslaved and ran away from the plantations to form their own settlements.
2. Royal Museums Greenwich, "The Story of the Windrush," https://www.rmg.co.uk/stories/windrush-histories/story-of-windrush-ship.

child," McClymont came to England in the late-1960s; a journey that she describes as "the shattering of an illusion of what it means to belong in the Mother Country" and which involved separation from her own mother, tenderly recounted in "Kool-Aid." Themes linked to migration, displacement, outsider-ness, discrimination and a sense of "unbelonging" abound, as the poems ebb and flow between the "things we choose to forget" ("Like buried treasure or fossils in rocks") and those that need to be brought into the light. Several poems that honour, for example, those whom Britain forgot, such as the British West Indian troops who fought for the "Mother Country" during the First and Second World Wars (in "Afrikan Remembrance Day" and "Mutiny in Taranto").

From Britain, the journey winds repeatedly back to contemporary Jamaica, as we are introduced to a whole host of characters drawn from family portraits and other life observations, creating often humorous portraits that sit alongside those that are deeply moving and spiritually inspired. In "The Shadows," we meet the *higgler* (a Jamaican female market trader) as she tries to find a bed for the night in an abandoned colonial house, only to find that its shadowy occupants still refuse her entry. It is these same ghostly power structures from the colonial past – still present, still controlling – that are brought to the fore in poems such as "Liquid sunshine" and "Sea breeze" where white tourists continue to lay claim to Jamaica as a playground for their paradisical fantasies.

Other poems bring to life the difficulties faced by the African Caribbean community now residing in Britain, which start at school and continue through adulthood. In "Word Glut," for example, a child is upbraided and punished for the simple act of writing and knowing too much, while in "Shoot for the Stars" another child is actively discouraged from achieving any of her ambitions. The same patterns follow the lives and careers of others, where invisible glass ceilings make it hard to gain promotion or recognition, as the "rules of the game" keep shifting (in "Blackleg").

In counterbalance are the many poems that pay homage to leading lights within Black, African and Caribbean communities – Marcus Garvey, Claude McKay, Langston Hughes, Maya Angelou – and exhort people to rise up against societal prejudice. For even if "Your ivory tower is off bounds to me […] I must walk unbent," continuing to "pound the pavements" to gain recognition (in "The

Ivory Tower"). More than just surviving, the poems speak of thriving. They walk with pride and celebrate achievement. In "A Girl Writes Back: Ode to Rudyard Kipling," we are transported from Jamaica to Britain, then to America and Ireland, witnessing the experiences that have informed the poet's writing, conveyed by the repeated refrain "If you can…" that marks the beginning of each stanza. The poem resolves with the voice of a motherly ancestor, who says, *if you can* do all this, "*Then, Putus, yuh is a ooman, mi dawta, An' tough enuff to walk dis far alone.*"

Last but not least is the skilful use of humour that brings much depth and humanity to the themes, scenes and characters portrayed. There is the short but brilliantly conveyed "Gaze on a Grecian Goddess" or the "Grumpy Old Man" with his long list of likes and dislikes, oscillating from the most sublime, "the constellations," all the way down to the most mundane: "He loathed his wife's blue rinses."

Closing with the sign of the rainbow in "Swan Lake Neck," *Walk-Foot Woman* is a collection that speaks from a place of authenticity about McClymont's journey as a poet who carries within her memories of the "walk-foot women" that came before. Like the remnants of a visionary dream, the conclusion to that opening poem sees the walk-foot woman tying seven strips of cloth from her plaid headtie to overhanging branches. The poet is leaving a trail for future writers to carve their own path through the ancestral forests of memories, history and identity, while always remembering and paying homage to those whose lives were lost to slavery.

Dr. Nicola Frith,
Senior Lecturer at the University of Edinburgh.

FOREWORD

Having written the foreword for Dr. McClymont's well-researched historical novel, *Little River*, it is my pleasure to endorse *Walk-Foot Woman and Other Poems*. Like a river that started as one drop of water, *Walk-Foot Woman* started with one poem in 1990, written by the poet when her daughter (Rebecca) was two-years-old. To its credit, this collection could be regarded as a little river of poems. Most of the titles relate to the historical contexts of the poems, stirring emotions when recalling the lives of our enslaved African ancestors.

Educated at a Baptist all-age school in rural Jamaica in the 1960s, and in England in the 1960s and '70s, Dr. McClymont uses poetry to write back to English literature (the "slabs of poetry" regurgitated at school in Jamaica). Consequently, the names of poets such as Charles Kingsley, John Masefield, Walter de la Mare and Robert Burns jump off the pages. At the same time, the collection attempts to humanise former enslaved Africans such as James Somerset (England) and Joseph Knight (Scotland). In an attempt to write her enslaved ancestors back into history, the poet reconstructs their lived reality in "Enemies of the Empire", "Calico Petticoat Rebellion", and "The Archway of No Return."

In *Walk-Foot Woman*, Dr. McClymont un/wittingly reveals her love of the Jamaican landscape and celebrates three national heroes: Paul Bogle, George William Gordon and Marcus Garvey. Like her muse, Claude McKay, she has a "a fierce hatred of injustice", which is evident in poems inspired by McKay, Garvey and Langston Hughes. Writing back to "the coloniser", there are poems to historical figures such as David Livingstone and Rudyard Kipling. Racial injustice runs through the collection like a roaring river; hence there is a nod to Meghan Markle and Prince Harry!

Like so many children who were born in the Caribbean, Dr. McClymont is a proud Windrush child. Consequently, she has drawn on this historical period in the collection. As a member of the Windrush Generation myself, I thank Dr. McClymont for allocating two poems to me, which I dedicate to my late dear mother and aunts who mothered and fathered me: "Ode to Joseph Knight and James Somerset", and "David Livingstone's Promised Land."

What is so captivating about *Walk-Foot Woman* is the overarching theme of journeying by land, air and sea. In terms of structure, the collection is divided into two parts and relies on different poetic styles to examine issues of race, gender, class, chattel slavery, colonisation, religion, migration, survival, dislocation and so on. Overall, the uniqueness of this collection is that the histories of so many different people are expressed through poetry.

Professor Sir Geoff Palmer OBE,
Chancellor of Heriot-Watt University, Scotland.

PART ONE
WALK-FOOT WOMAN

Walk-Foot Woman

Strolling through the glade, I picked up a stick
When a faint sound came from a clump of bushes,
Causing me to turn in the direction
From whence it came forth – to the east, I think.

"Whissh!" A smack rather like a *sibble jack*,[3]
Followed by: "*Yaso*,[4] *bandu*.[5] Yuh 'ave *quatty*?"[6]
"A who deh?" I called out, but no one made answer –
The voice survived as a faint echo from the past.

All at once, the *shame-a-macka*[7] leaves curled,
And closed on a breath of wind. "Touch mi not!"
The glade suddenly gave way to dense woodland
Where I left a trail for those who'd come after:

    I, the walk-foot woman,[8] tied seven strips
    Of my plaid headtie on random branches.

---

3. "Climbing shrub." *Sibble jack* was used in the old days to beat enslaved Africans. It is rather like a cane but is easier to bend. For more information on the Jamaican terms used in this collection, see F. Cassidy and R. Page, *Dictionary of Jamaican English* (Cambridge: Cambridge University Press, 2009).
4. "Over here."
5. "Headband." Tortoise shell *bandus* were popular in the 1960s.
6. "Silver coin." A *quatty* was worth one and a half pennies in colonial Jamaica.
7. "Chameleon grass."
8. A "walk-foot woman" was a female who walked everywhere because she had no other means of transport.

Pilgrim Stick

Woman, do you know who made you who you are?
I gave you knowledge when you were as innocent as a lamb,
Unbound your feet and taught you how to walk;
Gave you insight and opened your eyes to man's folly!

Woman, do you know who bore you in the Southern Wilds?
I gave you suckling at those engorged black breasts,
Clothed you when you were naked as an egg without a shell;
Gave you food for thought and a place to lay your head.

Woman, do you know who made those *dust tracks on the road*?
I gave you wanderlust and set you on your travels,
Walked behind you each time you looked over your shoulder;
Gave you a pilgrim stick to use in the heat and dust?

Woman, do you know who made you so unique?
I gave you staying power when others fell by the wayside,
Picked you up when you tripped over that stumbling block;
Gave you a map when the dream stealer stole your compass!

Woman, do you know who steered your ship in stormy seas?
I gave you courage when the hands on deck threw you overboard,
Rescued you when your lifeboat sank like a lead balloon;
Gave you a canoe when the sharks circled their bait?

Woman, do you know who guided your steps in the wilderness?
I gave you boldness when the pack wolves began to howl,
Walked before you when the fog descended like a shroud;
Gave you hope when the dream-seller sold you false promises?

Woman, do you know who made you so complete?
I gave you the gift of speech and a razor sharp tongue,
Commanded you to speak and to stand up for your rights;
Gave you visions when inspiration dried up like mother's milk.

The Change

It first came at Black Rock in Barbados
(Where the Bajans say, "Cheese on bread!"):
Dousing starched pillow case with its first deluge,
Dripping down my wet face *in the heat of the night.*

It came uninvited to Swansea Bay in Wales,
Cascading down back – forming sweatband 'round waist!
Sand between toes and Afro shrinking in the humidity,
Damping desire to visit Dylan Thomas' stomping ground.

It came flowing at Rodney Bay in St Lucia
Whilst hiking up to the fort on Pigeon Island:
Beads of perspiration springing up like well-water;
Shielding my eyes to see Martinique on a clear day.

It came unannounced on the subway in New York:
Rivulets running down each side of my face,
Drenching white linen tunic and matching slacks;
Knowing looks as train approached Grand Central.

It came unexpected at London's Royal Opera House,
Music floating above audience at the Ballet Black;
Fanning furiously with French concertina silk fan,
Moistness in-between the final curtain going down.

It came freely on a school reunion in Jamaica,
Breaking out and flowing like Dunn's River Falls.
Slinky silk slip clinging to curves and clammy skin;
Fan snapping shut and 'kerchief mopping up the spill.

It came suddenly at the Carlton Hotel in Dublin
In the midst of my first public performance there!
Hand-held fan and sympathetic gendered smiles,
Damp underarms and even damper insoles in shoes.

It came boldly at the Scottish Parliament in Edinburgh
Whilst discussing African women and climate change!
Eliciting empathetic nods and grimaces from the sistren,
Fifty-somethings heading towards that final drop of sweat.

The Mad Doctor of Edinburgh Castle

It stood on the slopes of a small mound,
Gazing up at the tree-capped hills above.
This monument to old Scotland was once
Home to an infamous redhead: Lewis Hutchinson!

Dubbed the mad doctor of Edinburgh Castle,
Flame haired Hutchinson tried to escape justice.
Ensnared by Admiral Rodney in Town Harbour,
He was sentenced to the gallows at Spanish Town.

Where once Hutchinson stood on the battlements,
Keeping watch over all his eyes could survey,
Wandering spirits now float on the evening breeze,
Calling to passers-by: "Howdy-do; howdy-do!"

Archaeologists trying to preserve this historic site
Whilst feeling the emotional residue of past pain,
Inflicted by the murderer of Edinburgh Castle
On misguided souls in fear of his power.

Edinburgh Castle, designated Heritage Site
(Built by a tyrant over two centuries ago),
Enjoying the peace and beauty of the landscape;
Carved out of lumps of stone with bare hands.

Displaced architecture eyeing the locals warily,
A decaying legacy of Britain's overseas empire:
Derelict and standing empty and abandoned,
Giving off an air of romantic decay in the hills.

Light flooding from a skyline in a passageway;
Shadows grouped in the darkness of despair.
Mangled bodies dumped in Hutchinson's Hole;
Memorials to the intrepid sojourners in the sun.

The Island of Springs: Ode to the West Wind

It's a hot land, the Island of Springs,
Full of black birds, *jankros*⁹ and guinea fowls!
I never ever see my island home
Without elation followed by tears of joy.

It's a fruited land, the Island of Springs,
Sour-sop and sweet-cup orchards blossom there
And the clouds hover above the cornfields.
There's cool breeze, and northern folk winter there.

Will you not come home, my generation?
It's spring and *gaulins*¹⁰ are in the pastures!
Blue is the sky, my generation;
And yellow is the colour of the sun.

The *John-to-whits*¹¹ are singing in the valleys.
It's clear sky, sunshine and soft rain at dawn.
It's music to my ears, to hear the *John-to whits*;
And see the hill springs welling up from the ground.

Parakeets are calling in the pimento trees.
So will you not come home, my generation,
And rest your feet on the Queen Mother's stool?'
Says my island, full of migrating birds.

It's the road to Drumilly I love to walk,
To the sleepy hamlet of Quashie Grass;
To the hilltop ruin of Edinburgh Castle
In the hot land, my island, where I truly belong.

---

9. "John Crows" or "vultures."
10. "Heron bird."
11. This refers to a black-whiskered song bird with an olive greenish colour.

Drumilly Remembered

Nestled in the orange valleys of St Ann
Lay the half-empty village of Drumilly.
Here a tiny hummingbird snores in slumber,
Unconcerned about the acute sense of absence.

In the hills you'll find farm hands hard at work:
Old men toiling on the poorest upland soil,
Young men harvesting without ploughing fields;
Youth rolling *ganja* with eyes as vacant as a ghost.

Like an elephant with a startling sneeze,
A stray dog sneezes grit from her nostrils.
Irritated by the sticky slug-slime on her mouth,
She has come to nature's buffet too late.

Yelping after a kick from a strong back foot,
The blow has struck the dog's under-belly!
Leaving aside her natural tendency to flee,
The big-bellied stray lies in a pool of blood.

Meantime bleached bones litter a nearby field
Where an errant heifer choked on an orange.
A year on, goat herds nibble invasive plants,
Some idly chewing down the undergrowth.

At midnight, a beam of light pierces the darkness
While four puppies lie in a bloody sack beneath
A canopy of trees (eyewitnesses) whose trunks
Had welded together down the centuries.

With a rejuvenating sneeze and a flap of ears,
The mother licks the lifeless puppies at dawn.
Sniffing, she walks away from nature's bounty,
Away from a black sunrise and circling vultures.

Moving Up

"It's very Romeo an' Juliet up 'ere."
Standing on a fabulous balcony,
Looking down from his penthouse in uptown
On humanity wallowing in poverty downtown.

"Yuh wahn a game of dominoes, brethren?"
He loved to open the French doors,
Holding a bottle of cold Red Stripe beer.
"Up 'ere, I can recite Shakespeare: *Julius Caesar*!"

"I come to bury Caesar, not to praise him."[12]
Surrounded by his domino-playing spars,
His gold watch outshone their off-the-peg jeans.
Ice rings dripped from his fingers. "Blood fiah!"

> The golden boy of hip-hop had arrived.
> "Tek a look at mi crib; mi moving up!"

---

12. From W. Shakespeare, *Julius Caesar*, Act 3, Scene 2.

A Better Future: Ode to Langston Hughes

What happens to ambition discouraged?
Does it retreat from formal instruction,
Does it reject negative thinking friends,
Or does it network and try to aspire?

What happens to ambition killed off?
Does it become the leader of the gang,
Does it "knife up" the rivals of friendship,
Or does it "shoot up" the more refined stuff?

What happens to ambition unfulfilled?
Does it lay dormant like seeds in the ground,
Does it shrivel up like dead autumn leaves,
Or does it smoulder on the fire of rage?

What happens to high ambition delayed?
Does it burn bright like a light in the dark,
Does it loiter on the streets of destiny,
Or does it fight for a better future?

If We Must Live

If we must live[13] to fulfil our hopes and aspirations,
Let it not be like men living of the edge of society,
Grown slack in zeal and getting by without great ideals.
Truant by trend and absent without paternal leave.

O kinsmen, let us agree to reject learned helplessness,
Fostered by dead men who devalued our human rights.
We stand complacent while foxes spoil the vines.
Yet our vines have tender grapes that yield fine wine.

If we must live in a time that endangers low expectations,
Tell our sons that they have a future worth fighting for.
Let them not knife each other at the first sign of conflict,
Or gun down blood brothers in the name of dis/respect!

O kinsmen, let us take positive action and set real goals:
Root out the guns and knives that kill our young vines!
Let our sons not spill their hot blood in pride and anger.
Let them not destroy their future with one death blow.

If we must live in a world where Black Lives Matter not
(Denied employment and blamed for social problems),
Let us stop scapegoating and blaming each other.
Raise our youth on the shoulders of *great expectations*!

O kinsmen, let us talk about hope and reparations.
Fight against racism, sexism and all forms of isms.
Tell our sons and daughters true success in not innate.
Seize opportunity and insert ourselves into the debate.

---

13. Inspired by Claude McKay's poem, "If We Must Die."

Insurmountable Heights: Ode to Marcus Garvey

If we must run the race of our lives,
Let it be on a level playing field
With all participants given a chance
To run with the winners like Usain Bolt!

If we must chew grass in our chosen fields,
Let us graze alongside the sheep and cows
And not stray from the straight and narrow path,
Plunging headlong over the precipice.

If we must excel in seats of learning,
Rubbing shoulders with Jim, Jack and Joe Bloggs,
Let us refuse to roost with the chickens
And fly like eagles above Mount Rushmore.

If we must scale insurmountable heights,
Let us make ready with our climbing ropes
And not hang off the ledge by our fingers,
Mouthing Garvey: "Up, up, you mighty race!"[14]

---

14. Inspired by Marcus Garvey's quotations.

The Ivory Tower: Ode to The White House

Your ivory tower is off bounds to me
And I am seething like the sizzling sun
But I have enough grace and good sense
To keep a still tongue in my muted mouth.

The paving stones have worn out my shoes
But I must keep a calm face as I walk
Past a white house manned by liveried men
With the fire of ambition burning within.

Alas, I must walk unbent with the thought that,
In the scramble for authority on my past,
I must not aspire to sit in seats of learning
Or intrude into the canon of men with beards.

> Lo! I must continue to pound the pavements,
> Fighting my foes for crumbs from your table.

The Shadows: Ode to Walter de la Mare

"Is dere anyone in?" called the *higgler*,[15]
Watching the full moon fall on the front door,
While her restless mule grazed on the wild grass
Of the cottage's fern-covered front yard.
Forest birds flew over the fig trees,
Above the spreading branches in the vale,
And she called out in a much louder voice:
"Is dere anyone in?" fist pounding the door.
Not a single soul stirred from their haunts within.
No prying faces behind the jalousie windows
Looked out to see her raised hand and dark face
Where she stood, curious and unmoving.
Eerily, a congregation of shadows
(That haunted the cobwebbed colonial cottage)
Glided around the one chair in the hallway,
And paused in the quietness to heed hooting owls,
Listening in the damp mouldy interior
To the bone-tired *higgler*'s throaty voice.
Wavering, she sensed their unseen presence,
The empty faces staring into her very soul,
While her mule halted, grazing on green leaves
Beneath the heady scent of wild flowers.
Then, quite suddenly, she straightened her back:
"Tell dem mi call an' nobody answa me,
Dat all mi wanted was *a cool bed*."
Not a shadow moved inside the cottage,
Though her gravelly voice sounded within,
Echoing in the dark eerie emptiness,
Falling on the shadows' earless ears.
Sure, they heeded her mule braying loudly,
And the clip-clop, clip-clop of hooves on gravel.
They heard the animal galloping off
As the *higgler* and her mule took to the dark country road.

---

15. "A female market trader or businesswoman." A *higgler* is usually a woman who walks from village to village with a basket on her head (selling fruit and vegetables) or a suitcase (selling women's underwear and toiletries).

Liquid Sunshine

On a far off sunny shoreline in the tropics,
A gentle wind caresses the Queen of the Carib.
The rosy-cheeked dawn blushes at the amorous sun,
Mounting the naked hills and slipping into the valleys.

Itsy-bitsy, teenie-weenie, white bikinis on golden sand;
Buxom black babes bouncing up big booties at bars.
Jamaica shaking her honey-covered stick at tourists
Enjoying the morning sun on their tattooed backs!

On a far off sunny shoreline in the tropics,
Speedos and cupped swimwear "uglying up" poolsides!
Swim-up bars serving Appleton and Red Stripe beer;
Blue-black bartenders bantering about "a better break."

European towels tossed territorially across loungers,
As if they were laying claim to the Holy Land!
A sudden downpour of liquid sunshine at noon,
Waves hammering at the rocks and the seawall.

On a far off sunny shoreline in the tropics,
White weddings and a slice of paradise on offer:
Pale-skinned brides wrapped in enchanting beauty;
White teeth black womanhood serving champagne.

Fun-seekers gyrate on cruising catamarans,
Oblivious to the hills draped in green foliage.
Coconut vendors peddle water jelly on the beach
Where mosquitoes lurk like blood-sucking vampires.

On a far off sunny shoreline in the tropics,
The reddish tint of a sunset smudges the skyline.
Sun-seekers abandon themselves to the moment:
A little spliff to smoke out the departing day.

Potbellied men energised by the touch of the sun,
Oldies swimming against the tide in knotted silk ties,
Under-forties hanging out at bars with ripped biceps,
Poker-face Brit fizzing with ideas for a new book.

Black Forest Gateaux

"I'm blessed to have a man like *Tony-C*,"
Said the wife, clutching a Louis Vuitton bag
And a pair of red bottomed shoes.
"Oh fudge! I can't walk in sky-scraper heels."

"So Kate – that's what they're called – Louboutin's."
The personal shopper's voice dropped in the store
Where shoes sold at sixty pounds and upwards.
"Did you sign a pre-nup? Men are so fickle."

"I'm heading south to warmer weather soon…"
The wife was aware of what was to come,
But handsome meant good-looking daughters
And catwalks. "My house needs a makeover."

"Again! It's hardly a hovel, Sugar."
The personal shopper chose Jimmy Choo,
Experiencing a fleeting vision
Of Rodin's *The Kiss* on a shelf. "You're quiet."

"We're off to our Barbados retreat…"
The ex-model adjusted her beige pashmina,
Enjoying the high life in wealthy row.
"Why do trousers look better on black bottoms?"

"Blacks trying to rise above their social status."
The personal shopper eyed two social climbers,
Tossing their thick mane and flashing gold cards.
"Next they'll be dressed up to be seen at Henley."

"Don't forget Ascot and the Derby – you're racist,"
Said the wife, whipping out her Mastercard.
"We all want to dress to blend in with our betters."
The cash register broke the silence. *Kerching*!

"I'm not racist, Sugar. I only date mixed-race guys,"
Said a voice, piqued and dreaming of a stately pile.
"My mother once said, 'No brown grandchildren!'
If you can't find a pure Englishman, stay single!'"

"Cream tea and scones at the Grosvenor next?"
The wife allowed her true nature to escape.
"I quite fancy a slice of Black Forest gateaux.
Decadent! Oh cripes! A pound on the hips."

Sea Breeze

Too cocooned to have suffered the miseries
Of having the wrong pigmentation of skin,
They waded into the sparkling water
Under the eye of adult supervision.

"My Bonnie lies over the ocean, my Bonnie…"
Above, a tropical sky with laugher and mirth.
Below, treading sea-water unsupervised
In the sunny realms guarded by childhood.

Tanning beached bodies from the First World,
With their silent glances and roaming eyes.
Enough to induce indigestive anxiety
At the fast food bar on the powdery sand.

Bunches of coconuts on palm fringed beach
Brought down by a homeless loitering youth,
Trying to make a quick American dollar
From a fat, pale Texan in Dacron shorts.

Doing his very best to jolly things along,
A paunchy Brit sourcing gags for his next show,
Cursing his agent for not getting him
A plum role in the Christmas pantomime.

"You mustn't stand too near to the ropes, Sam."
A dauntingly full cruise ship bobbed on the waves,
Voyeurs craving a slice of paradise with cocktails,
Waving languidly from the decks and portholes.

Not familiar with table etiquette at sea,
The hoi-polloi rushed the sumptuous buffet
Like "hooligans at a feast" for a prince,
Committing a *faux pas* on their first voyage.

Waving frantically at the Sea Breeze cruiser,
A tiny blob surfaced in the water momentarily.
He had strayed away from the roped area
And disappeared under the waves of the day.

"There's someone in the water. I saw him!"
Sinking fast and dragged down by the current,
The watchful eyes of adult supervision
Snoozed under the influence of fire water.

Bantering and ogling white skin turned brown,
A well-oiled lifeguard, looking rather urgent,
Extricated himself from the eye-candy
With their wash-board bellies and legs eleven.

"Mi lose di likkle wuk to bombo-claat!"[16]
Hearing the shriek of a distraught mother,
Who had lost sight of her son in the sea,
The scales fell from his eyes. "Lawd, mi job!"

---

16. This is a Jamaican cultural expression, meaning "I (Mi) lose (have lost) my job (di likkle wuk) to bombo-claat (sanitary towel term used during slavery)."

"Heart of Oak"

When I see bamboo trees swaying from left to right,
Across the skyline with their shooting branches,
I think of black-eyed pandas gorging on the stalks.

When I see banana leaves quivering in the breeze,
Water-logged trees taking a hurricane battering,
I think of bunches bearing a thousand green fingers.

When I see cactus plants with their pointed tips,
Growing profusely on "a green hill far away",
I think of *Our Native Son* growing up in Sunnyville.

When I see breadfruit leaves shuddering in the wind,
In a vale where the river "murmurs and meanders",
I think of Captain Blyth and *Mutiny on the Bounty*.

When I see yam vines trailing on javelin poles,
Boasting yam names like *afu*, yellow, soft and white,
I think of Roger Mais: "All Men Come to the Hills..."[17]

When I see poinsettia flowers, blood-red at Christmas,
Decorating hallways to welcome the Yuletide,
I think of three wise men following a lone star.

When I see oak trees growing in English cities,
I think of the Royal Navy on the seas, men singing:
"Heart of oak are our ships; heart of oak are our men..."

---

17. "All Men Come to the Hills" is a poem by Roger Mais and can be found in J.E.C. McFarlane (editor), *A Treasury of Jamaican Poetry* (London: University of London Press, 1949).

Eight Rivers

The night jasmine wafts her scent
On the tropical breeze,
While sturdy South Sea roses sprout
In an invisible realm of fragrance and odours.

Here the aroma of woodland orchids
Brings on a foot-stamping sneeze
And African marigolds flower
Their hearts out in the bush.

Drums beat beneath a tropical moon,
While field-hands seek temporary escape.
The Kumina Queen plants her feet firmly
On the ground, connecting with Earth's energy.

Against this back-breaking backdrop,
The sun rises over a limp dew-laden land,
Glistening on green foliage like gems
On garments in a theatre in the round.

Over the corrugated iron roofs,
A flock of parakeets take flight,
Landing in a gummy lignum vitae tree
Where a sun-warming chameleon lurks.

In the sky, two hawks plunge downwards
In a menacing show of might!
In the river, a shoal
Of fresh fish feast on fallen fruit in a frenzy.

Across the ocean, Mother Africa's
Laugh shatters the sorrow.
Her lost child, Kofi, toils under
A new sun with a new name: Don.

Calm and distinguished looking, my mistress
Gathers rose petals for her toilet water.
On the Isle of Streams,
Eight rivers meet without a leg to stand on.

Footprints Upon Our Souls

When the years have ravaged our features
And swarming locusts have eaten our crops,
Think not of the stolen hours of hard graft,
But only of the rough cobblestone street
Where we put down roots in the prime of life.
Don't look back and envy your youthful self
Or worry about what folk think of you,
Blaming your misdeeds on your conditioning,
For time has left its footprints upon our souls
Like hand-prints in pre-historic cave art.
Let's select the memories worth keeping
And shed those that hurt us like sticks and stones.

> When the winter has come and our joints ache,
> Think only that we loved and we lived well.

Fossils in Rocks

The things we choose to forget are many:
Whether appointments and anniversaries,
The birthdays of friends, families and foes,
Or the *bully-sticks* that made schooldays hell.

The things we choose to forget are many:
Never mourning the deaths of those Goliaths,
Bosses who refused to acknowledge us,
Or the slingshots that slew our enemies.

Why return to the scenes of past battles,
With the flames of war burning in our eyes,
When return will only open old wounds
That have festered, scabbed and healed with time?

> The things we forget should remain dormant,
> Like buried treasure or fossils in rocks.

David Livingstone's Promised Land

Africa, they said, was the Dark Continent,
Though the landscape was lush and verdant.
Sunny fountains rolled down Victoria Falls
And the bushman bowed down to wood and stone.

Africa, they said, was an intoxicating place
Devoid of Christianity, commerce and civilisation
(No clothes, shoes, cooking pots, pans, clocks, pianos):
A land of bubbling cauldrons and fleshpots.

Africa, they said, was beguilingly seductive!
Darkest Africa, Livingstone's promised land:
"His body was hung over a tree to dry,
Embalmed and shipped back to England."

Africa, they said, had no ancient monuments:
No Coliseum to match Rome's might,
No Parthenon to rival the glory of Greece;
No Great Wall of China to keep invaders out!

Africans, the wise men in robes of white said,
Did not have the technologies "that we have",
Produced "nothing great in art or science..."[18]
Had written nothing worth reading – no Latin!

Africa, I said, before the Transatlantic Trade
(Reading my way into the contentious subject),
Had her own empires – Mali, Songhai, Akan,
Not to mention the great library of Timbuktu.

---

18. See the works of philosophers such as Immanuel Kant, Edward Long and David Hume.

Afrikan Remembrance Day

"We will remember" – how could we forget
Black poppy rose as a symbol of respect?
Marking Afrikan Remembrance Day –
Tribute-paying to those who laid down lives.

Saluting the fallen with our lapel pins:
Courageous soldiers and unsung heroes;
Children of the dust who fought and died
For the "amnesia-prone" Mother Country.

Commonwealth wreath-laying at the Cenotaph,
Celebrating our heroes with hymns and harps,
Recalling their contributions to the Great War,
Making the ultimate sacrifice for their King:

> British West Indies Regiment, the King's
> African Rifles and African Frontier Force.

Barbed Wire on the Western Front

Drums beating, army marching on its stomach,
Whistles blowing across the hills of time.
Piper playing morale-boosting tunes;
Death marching on foot to glory, oh glory!

Forward and onward to no man's land,
Horses' hooves trampling the King's highway.
Machine guns spitting out silver bullets;
German artillery barraging the British.

Twilight ebbing on the Western Front,
Men haemorrhaging blood in the trenches.
Life departing on the wings of the night;
Soldiers sleeping in death in deep dugouts.

> Flags flying on barbed wire with steely thorns,
> Union Jack fluttering – patterned with bullets!

The Call to Action

"Your King and country need you."
A handful of slogans had stowed away
To the tropics on a banana boat:
"The Empire Needs Men! The Overseas States."

When Duke Robinson joined the British West
Indies Regiment his boyish dreams came through:
The flights of fancy, seeing himself in uniform,
Poised and playing his part for the war effort.

"Join together. Train together. Fight together."
England, the *backras*[19] had said with great pride,
Was lovingly known as the Mother Country;
Germany was the iron-fisted Fatherland.

Duke did not question why one poster
Depicted Germany with bloodstained hands,
Showing an ape-like German in a helmet;
Or why four allies joined forces against the Kaiser.

"There is still a place in the line for you."
Answering the call to action was twofold:
The war was a way of avenging past wrongs
And driving a bayonet through the Fatherland.

For unemployed men like Duke, the Great War
Meant regular pay and respect at home
Where he intended to build a new life
With the sweetheart he called Miss Sugar-Foot.

"Forward! Forward to victory! Enlist now!"
Duke's great-grandfather, Abba, had come up
From slavery and died "of want" in freedom –
Far better to die for a noble cause!

---

19. "White men."

"Pack up your troubles in your old kit bag..."[20]
Sixty-six percent of Jamaican men (10,280)
With exceptional physique and excellent discipline.
"Laaaawd! Labour duty on di Western Front."

---

20. Felix Powell's World War I marching song (1915). For more information, see "Pack up your troubles," firstworldwar.com: a multimedia history of world war one, www.firstworldwar.com.

Mutiny in Taranto: Ode to Mr James Fairweather

"Chi-bum! Lawd, di bumb dem a com' dung!"[21]
The bones of a dead soldier, Duke Robinson,
Lay in a neglected corner of New Castle.
"Lawd, di bumb dem a com' dung! Boom-boom!"

"They shall not grow old…" The dead soldier's son,
Festus, held a keepsake of *The Times*: September
Nineteen Fourteen. "Robert Lawrence Bunyan."
The veteran sighed, "Ode to Remembrance."

"Papa answa di call durin' di Great War."
Festus' voice fell on the hollowness in the room,
Living out his golden years in a care home.
Outside, a gardener raked the freshly mown lawn.

"Chi-bum!" The World War II veteran chanted.
His father's regiment stocked shells at Ypres,
Stretcher bearing on the battlefield of Flanders.
"Som' get court martial fi mutiny in Taranto."

"Papa serve in Palestine. Aye sah! Courage sleepin'
In di rain widout cover. Nurse, weh mi poppy?"
Skull face care-giver pinning on red rosette.
"Papa dig latrines in Taranto. Bleurgh!"

"London", Papa said, "went wild wid excitement
In nineteen eighteen: Victory parade, Empire troops.
Dem com' in di t'ousands but not di BWIR[22] –
Not welcome! Left, right, left…'ear di trumpet…"

"I serve in di Royal Air Force – ground crew."
Memories of wartime flew through Festus' head.
"I go 'ome after di war – no future in Jamaica.
I com' back on di Windrush wid Lord Kitchener."

---

21. "Lord, the bombs are coming down."
22. The British West Indies Regiment (BWIR). For more information, see the Imperial War Museum, "The Story of the British West Indies Regiment in the First World War," https://www.iwm.org.uk/history/the-story-of-the-british-west-indies-regiment-in-the-first-world-war.

"Some of mi comrades sleeping in eternal darkness."
There was an urgency to put his story on paper.
"Colonel Lipton was my MP in Lambeth in di '50s…
Nurse, turn up di TV – time fi East Enders."

Ration Books in Battersea

It wasn't like this in my day, the war years:
Hands springing up like mushrooms in schoolrooms,
Bombed and evacuated to the Kent countryside;
Pink cheeked lasses hop-picking in cotton smocks.

Aye! Churchill ate a chicken for breakfast each day.
The government urged women to "make do and mend,"
Gravy browning on white legs with thin pencil lines,
Ration books – powdered eggs for tea again.

The winds of change blew over post-war Battersea.
Coloured men in bunkers on Clapham Common!
Prefab homes a stone's throw from Falcon Road,
Hastily built to ease the borough's housing crisis.

Paper thin walls and flimsy fibreglass curtains,
Flat roofs riddled with killer asbestos.
Our kid marvelling at the magic of television,
Eavesdropping on the world from a saggy sofa.

Saturday afternoon cinema in drainpipes.
Bubble gum on seats at Granada theatre.
Switchblades and knuckle dusters on Cedars Road.
Catholic choir boys shaking like quivering sea grass.

Fag-Ash Lil in sponge rollers on Queen's Town Road,
Admiring her old man's new motorbike with side-car.
Teddy boys with quiffs and blue suede shoes,
Hopping *On the Buses* going *Up the Junction*.

Stout West Indian women hogging the sidewalk,
Doing their weekly shopping on the Northcote Road;
Clutching their stash of Green Shield stamp books,
Crowding the post office with monthly remittances.

Revisiting South London for old time's sake:
Skyscrapers, concrete, steel and glass tower blocks;
Harding & Hobbs land-marking Clapham Junction;
Battersea Power Station belching out grey clouds.

Buying on the "never never" whilst on the Nat King Cole.
Shopping for school uniform at Thorne's, Northcote Road.
Monied folk hopping on trains to Army & Navy, Victoria,
Exiting Clapham Junction Station like swarms of bees.

Men in the bookies crowding around the goggle box,
Watching Jackie Pollo, Big Daddy & Giant Haystacks!
Coloured families hunkering down on Lavender Hill,
Changing the complexion of Battersea in the Sixties.

"No Coloureds, No Irish, No Dogs"

Buoyed by the hope of a better future,
They packed grips[23] and donned felt hats:
Young men facing destiny head on,
Walking down the gangway at Tilbury.

Anticipation built up on the sea voyage,
But the cold heart of the city greeted them!
Front doors slamming in weary dark faces:
"Sorry, no coloureds, no Irish, no dogs."

Walking the streets of London by gaslight,
Snow and ice ravaging two male faces.
Hard lines appearing at the corners
Of youthful mouths in the winter months.

It seemed the damp days would never end:
Hail stones and rain battering leaky roofs;
Darkness beginning to win over light;
Underground trains rumbling like thunder.

At the end of another night shift,
They lay their heads on musty pillows,
Waking at mid-morning to a new day,
Heeding the call of the rag-and-bone man.

Listening to new footsteps on the landing,
They got up and lit the paraffin heater,
Warming their hands over the blue flame.
Dog barking! Irish family moving in next-door.

Notting Hill Carnival was their stomping ground:
An opportunity to let their guard down after work,
Tough macho men with steel in their black biceps.
Young blood getting mixed-up in "razor cut ups."

---

23. An old-fashioned burgundy cardboard suitcase, like those carried by the Windrush passengers.

No More Dreams to Chase

He dreams of days that are no more,
Butchering beef and seeing blood and gore.

She poses for the camera with arms akimbo,
Mouthing her song: "Sitting here in limbo."

He likes to sing to her, "I love sixpence…"
Keeping their greedy beneficiaries in suspense.

Ratbats make a racket in the roof at night,
Scuttling around with no more battles to fight.

Their weekly pension posted without delay,
So little time and the hours turn to a new day.

Their days are gone and they can't keep apace,
Exiting the race with no more dreams to chase.

The Kentuckian King of Boxing

Muhammad Ali shuffled across our screens
In the days of teenage spots and "break outs,"
Ranting about racism and a whiter shade of
White in the beauty pageants of the day.

Holding his big fist against his opponents
(Stripped of his WBA and WBC titles in 1970),
Ali, in 1974, brought Brixton to a standstill,
Motivating the African diaspora like no other.

One of the greatest boxers of all time,
Ali used his fame to motivate "the oppressed,"
Excluded from the great American Dream
By a giant network of power and privilege.

Lending his voice to the fight for Civil Rights,
Ali refused to join the Army shown on celluloid.
Conscientious objector to the Vietnam War,
Refusing to slaughter lives on religious grounds.

Facing jail with the underbelly of America,
Ali did not throw in the towel of anger
When his boxing license was lawfully revoked;
He took on the architects of segregation!

A heavy weight champion, he used his clout
To hold up a mirror to white America,
Calling out racial injustice in the land that
Lionised him as Olympic Boxing Champion.

Four times married with a stable of daughters,
Ali defied the odds to fulfil his dreams.
"Rumble in the Malaysian jungle" with his arch
Rival, Joe Frazier. "I am the greatest!"

Ali, the poet boxer, inspired a generation
Of restless Black British youth to dream big
(Chris Eubank, Frank Bruno, David Haye…),
Using their fists to negate their ascribed place.

Cassius Clay, the boy from Kentucky, threw his
Former slave name into the dustbin of history,
Rejected the Euro-American slave religion
And insisted on the right to name himself: Ali!

They came in their thousands to pay tribute,
Hailing the King of Boxing via social media,
Sky News, TV documentaries and pall bearers!
Men in Black: Will Smith, Tyson, Lennox Lewis…

Brooklyn Heights

Riding the crowded subway in Brooklyn Heights,
Conspicuous consumers clutch their pocket-books
With sly civility and frozen faces like masks,
Harbouring an inherent hostility towards difference.

Ousted from digs in *Going to Meet the Man*,[24]
Baldwin's Peter returns to Harlem's embrace.
Here, rheumy-eyed old Southerners croon Gershwin's
"Summertime,"[25] reliving the great Migration North.

Raising a smile at a calico queen beside the bar,
The wanderer sips whisky at Small's Paradise,
Fuming about his expulsion from the Heights.
"Your door is shut against my tightened face…"[26]

Home to Harlem,[27] working gals click-clack
Their way down Lenox Avenue in stilettos,
Seeking libertines to dance the Charleston
On floors the size of a postage stamp.

Whites born 'neath the shadow of Brooklyn Bridge,
Doing the Black Bottom under Prohibition,
Whisky in bottles wrapped with newspaper,
Home at dawn to a lamp post on Park Avenue.

On a street corner, a Northerner strums his banjo,
Vying for premium space, crooning "Old Zip Coon."
In a casino, bleary-eyed men in two-tone brogues
Roll the dice, humming "Luck be a lady tonight!"[28]

---

24. J. Baldwin, *Going to Meet the Man* (New York: Vintage, 1965).
25. Aria composed by George Gershwin in 1934 for the opera, *Porgy and Bess* (1935).
26. From Claude McKay's Poem, "The White House," https://aaregistry.org/poem/the-white-house-by-claude-mckay/.
27. Claude McKay, *Home to Harlem* (New York: Harper and Bros, 1928).
28. Lyrics written by Frank Loesser in 1950. This song was featured in the musical *Guys and Dolls* (1955).

Ride the dreary subway to *The Dinner Party*[29]
Uptown – Exhibition at Brooklyn Museum.
The "guests of honour"? Sappho, Boadicea
And thirty seven s/heroes dine on veal.

Ho! How comes Sojourner Truth is the only Soul
Sister favoured with a named place setting?
Aha! Nine hundred and ninety other s/heroes
Inscribed in gold letters on Heritage Floor.

---

29. Feminist artist Judy Chicago's "The Dinner Party" is a permanent exhibition at Brooklyn Museum, New York.

The Way West

As the seasons turn from spring to summer
(Autumn tumbling down England's leafy lanes),
Pioneers sail "*Westward ho!*" on the Mayflower,
Finding themselves in a new and alien world.

Hardy lumberjacks roaring "*Timber ho!*"
Men building log cabins by the Great Lakes,
Trading with the red man in his moccasins,
Soon to *become The Last of the Mohicans*.[30]

Fur trappers and grizzly bears on snow ridges.
Herds of buffalos roaming on the prairies.
Forts trading whiskey and yards of yellow ribbon.
Pony Express and free-spirited Stagecoach Mary.[31]

"*Howgh!*" Mustangs thundering over the Plains.
Cochise, Crazy Horse, Geronimo and Sitting Bull,
Swallowing "Bad medicine" before signing treaty;
Smoke signals and chiefs passing the peace pipe.

"*We come in peace.*" Cheyenne, Cherokee, Sioux
(Noble savages dressed in feathered war bonnets),
Deceived by "white eyes" with "forked tongues":
Totems and headdresses confined to reservations.

Gunfight at Apache Pass and *Comanche Creek*;
Scalping and Braves shooting "*Arrow in the Dust.*"
Native Americans relocated for a patch of earth.
Eye-water cascading in "The Vale of Tears."

---

30. J. F. Cooper, *The Last of the Mohicans: A Narrative* (Philadelphia: H.C. Carey & I. Lea, 1826).
31. Stagecoach Mary, or Black Mary, refers to Mary Fields (1832–1914), the first African American mail carrier. For more information, see Erin Blakemore, "Meet Stagecoach Mary, the Daring Black Pioneer Who Protected Wild West Stagecoaches," 11 August 2023, https://www.history.com/news/meet-stagecoach-mary-the-daring-black-pioneer-who-protected-wild-west-stagecoaches.

Wagon trains, Winchesters, catalogue women,
Saloons, fist fights, calico queens and tin stars.
Saddle tramps, cow punching, horse trading.
Barbed wire fences, stampedes and cattle barons.

Wells Fargo stagecoaches passing ghost towns.
Dynamite blowing asunder the Black Hills!
The Way West paved by Union Pacific railroad.
Gold rush and Forty-Niners singing "Clementine."

Home on the range with Mr and Mrs Granger –
White Protestant family born in Cochise County.
Kitchen ruled by Sunbonnet Sue and Hop-Sing,
Lauded for his roast turkey on Thanksgiving Day.

Neighbourhood Watch

"Hello. Who opened the gate and let you in?"
His paws made no sound on the wooden floor
But his toenails were a dead giveaway.
"Down, boy. Good boy. Off you go. Out you go."

Two days later, the dog stood on the path:
A large tan and cream pit bull terrier
Bared his canines and growled at her,
Salivating as if he smelled raw meat.

"What do you expect when you're wearing black?"
The dog's master resembled a meerkat,
Though his red face pictured a garden gnome.
"He likes a good sniff – nice little black dress."

Flushed, the woman ignored the roving eyes
When the dog's ears went back submissively.
Smiling, she took control of his leather lead.
"Good boy, Buddy. You need to feel useful."

"Settlin' in okay, is ya?" asked garden gnome,
Studying a removal van reversing
Into the quiet cul-de-sac: "Flaming nig-nogs!
The black minstrel show. I'm not having this!"

Brexit; Or Peddling Hyperbole

"They ought to go back to where they came from."
He sighed, taking a coffee break in the staff canteen.

"All this rhetoric about refugees welcome – poppycock!"
She said. "They've turned Calais into a jungle."

"We have the right to keep undesirables out."
He surfed the internet. "Flaming foreigners in lorries."

"UKIP is beginning to win me over." She sipped tea.
"I'm concerned about David Cameron's leadership and…"

"Farage is only good for a pint at the Rose and Crown…"
He fumed. "Comrade Corbyn is a train spotter – anorak."

"The Poles are coming over in long ships like Vikings."
She checked her watch. "It's plain sailing for them."

"I'm definitely throwing my hat into the Brexit ring."
He leered at the Play Girl of the Month on his laptop.

"Do you think I need a boob job and botox?"
She noted his silence. "What about us Brits?"

"Sod those tartan-clad Scots and the whining Welsh."
He scoured the internet. "Dublin is good for a stag do…"

"The Welsh are sore because Thatcher closed the mines.
And those *porridge wogs* wanted to break up the Union."

"I wouldn't mind being bossed about by Nicola Sturgeon."
He grinned. "Feisty lady in red. Energy ball – *Braveheart*!"

"Urgh! Alex Salmond's bushy eyebrows." She slurped tea.
"I need a key-note speaker to close the diversity conference."

"Take it up with my secretary. Peddling hyperbole is my forte."
He winked. "*Dinner Date* at yours? I love that programme."

"I could murder a curry from the local Indian takeaway," She let slip. "Tonight? I thought you said your wife…"

"Seriously, Brexit will affect all our jobs and the economy." His face was as calm as a mill pond. "The pound will fall."

"Cameron will fall on his sword for this – Gove at the helm." She sipped. "Boris? No way! Theresa May is a steady hand."

Diaspora Daughters of Africa

"Savages! Barbarians! Those backward brutes!"
Judgement was pronounced on the continent
By the pony-tail wearing man on the move.
"If Belgium was still in charge of the Congo…"

"It's those uneducated, beastly aunts!"
Unbridled words escaped the London Councillor,
Bowels turning at the thought of a blunt razor.
"Those Congolese treat their girls like bush meat."

"I think we need to police our language,"
Cautioned the race-conscious sister with twists,
Placing a heavy emphasis on *lan-guage*.
"Tolerance is key, and cultural sensitivity."

"We can't have children falling through the cracks."
Tweed jacket's porcelain cheeks reddened,
Delving deep into twists' lesser known views.
"The question is this, which side are you on?"

"Women's oppression under patriarchy is…"
Longing for some intellectual jousting,
Burn-your-bra advocate's heavy breasts sagged.
"Conspiring against a woman's right to say no is…"

"Some people are not fit to raise children."
Diploma-clad disciple of Babylon had
Assimilated into the team from hell.
"We need more BME foster parents to…"

"The focus on FGM sounds like reality avoidance."
Tribal war broke out between degree cap
And diploma – "diaspora daughters of Africa."
"You're points scoring. If the cap fits, wear it."

"Crikey! A car crash is on the cards, chaps."
Twin-set grew tired of the cat and mouse game,
Stamping the point home in kitten-heeled shoes.
"Ladies, leave your differences at the door."

"Has anyone seen that FGM awareness cake?"
Diploma turned to the torso of a black woman
On exhibition in Snow White's Sweden.
"Genital mutilation cake cutting. Gross."

"The Swedish minister of culture was unwise…"
Pony-tail head cut the throat of the mob,
Tailing off. "Ah, yes. King Leopold eating his
Chocolate cake. Once you go native there's no…"

Shoot for the Stars

"What are your plans for the future, Carol?"
Miss P hummed "The Happy Wanderer Song."[32]

"I'd like to be an air stewardess or a librarian, Miss,"
Carol said, addressing the career teacher.

"A librarian? That's for spinsters in cardigans, dear."
Miss P smiled, making notes on a blank sheet of paper.

"I wish I could be a pilot and fly around the world."
Carol lowered her eyes. "I'd love to fly a jet plane."

"Don't fly too close to the sun or you'll get burnt,"
Miss P advised. "You'll get your wings singed like Icarus."

"Perhaps a social worker, or maybe a teacher, Miss."
Carol hesitated. "I help my sisters with homework."

"Decisions, decisions: air hostess, pilot or librarian?"
Miss P asked. "Social work is out of your depth."

"I was good at Maths, English and Science at home."
Carol felted intimidated by a pair of dead eyes.

"This is England, dear. How about retail, Woolworths?"
Miss P sneered. "Auxiliary nursing is right up your street."

"Father says nursing is for those who can't do better."
Carol sniffed. "Perhaps a secretary in a bank, Miss."

"Secretarial work is for the more attractive girls, dear,"
Miss P chortled. "Banking is out of your league."

"Why can't I stay on at school and sit my A levels?"
Carol asked. "I want to go to university like the white…"

"Carol Proudfoot, you are a time squanderer.
I think you'd make a good Xerox operator."

---

32. Song written by Florenz Friedrich Sigismund (1788–1857).

"Xerox? Isn't that a photo-copying machine?" Carol frowned. "Oh well, I'll just be an actress."

"Frankly, you might as well shoot for the stars." Miss P gurned. "It'll all end in tears. You'll see."

"Blackleg"

Try asking your boss for a promotion,
Hinting about shattering glass ceilings,
Clutching the equality and diversity handbook,
Seeking advice from your shop steward,
Yet refusing to go on strike with the Union.
Hanging back from the pack like a lone wolf,
You will be branded "blackleg" and "scab"
For daring to cross the picket line solo.
You'll be accused of stirring up bad feelings,
Sent on team-building exercise with colleagues:
Away day to change behaviour and attitude,
Fraught with the danger of paintball bruises!

    Sent to Coventry for "out-thinking" your superiors,
    And othered for not knowing the rules of the game.

Word Glut

Miss did not believe in dishing out "*As*",
The teacher with the bob and bluest eyes.
She gave twenty-five out of twenty-five,
Saying "*As*" were for exceptional pupils.

Determined to succeed, I over-reached,
Burning the midnight oil until day break,
Digesting English literature at the table,
Claiming the right to aspire and inspire.

Miss did not believe I wrote that essay,
Blotting my copy book with inky thumbs,
Crossing through sentences with a biro,
Rewriting and restructuring paragraphs.

"You write too much under exam conditions."
Miss had marked me down for "word glut",
Saying I'd used two extra sheets of paper
To critique a *Midsummer Night's Dream*.

Diversion Tactics

"Your English is very good – sharp thinking!
About 'the main report', let it stand – *stet*."
He crossed his legs in his leather club chair.
"It really is rather good for a darkie…"

"Cometh the hour, cometh the (wo)man, eh?"
Quietly flamboyant in paisley socks,
He resorted to classic diversion tactics:
"Hark at you, clever clogs. You're a dark horse."

"I say, where did you learn to write like that?"
He exhaled the St. Bruno tobacco: "Quite a girl, eh?
Convent school! Were you born here?
Jamaica! The natives are restless there…"

    Smiling, he fondled the phallic-shaped pipe
    With a twinkle in his eye: "Capital!"

One of Us

"You're not like other coloured people, May,"
She said, studying my dark skin, "Are you?
I mean, you don't behave like them, do you?"
She scrutinised me in mid-sentence:
"You're different. You're like one of us."

"No offence, May, but you don't sound like them."
Stumped, she tripped over the words on her tongue:
"You know what I'm trying to say, don't you?
Seriously though, you don't act black. Oops!"
She squirmed, sensing the tension in the air.

"I'm not racist. I'm just clumsy with words,"
She dug herself into a deeper hole,
Adding, "It's not as if I said something offensive
Like nig-nog, darkie or sunshine, is it?"

Mistaken Identity

"There's no paper in the loo. Are you the cleaner?"
The academic gathered up tissue paper like a gleaner.

"Are you the manager of this poxy laundrette?"
The irate Irish traveller lit an illicit cigarette.

"Are you the shop assistant? Oh dear, ever so sorry."
The two Indian women suddenly sounded rather jolly.

"Are you the supply teacher? Oh fig! Is that a mole?"
The receptionist turned red, rummaging in her pigeonhole.

"Are you the care assistant? Poo! I nipped my pinky."
The nurse's pubescent breasts were rather perky.

"Excuse me, Miss. Are you the cashier?"
She squashed her Indian accent, stylish Mrs Bashir.

Bread Basket: Ode to Maya Angelou

"I hate to let my guard down."
She looked for a friendly face in the room.
"Even for a tick! I wish I could relax.
I can't be lax! What can I say?
Except that I hate to let my guard down."

"I lost my temper once and shouted out,
Opening my eyes and speaking loudly.
I think I was riled by a time waster.
I repeat, I hate to let my guard down."

"A clock of mine was filched by a time thief.
It had a gold face and Roman numerals.
I'll never forgive her and believe me,
I really hate to let my guard down."

"Now, if I felt that way about a time thief
What would I feel about that book stealer?
I ain' funning! My books are my bread basket!
And, I mean, I really hate to let my guard down."

The Pearl Necklace: Ode to The Daffodils

I rambled solitary as an oyster
That closes its shell when threatened undersea!
When all at once I sighted it again,
A string of lustrous pearls made into a necklace,
Beside the sea, beneath the waters,
Floating and moving with the ocean's current,
Cultured from a mussel or a clam,
And not the so-called grain of sand.
They strayed along the margins of a coral reef,
Sixty and six saw I at first sight,
Twisting and writhing like an eel.

The coral beneath them moved, but they
Outdid the pink and red shells in zeal.
A deep-sea diver could not be dizzy
In finding such a precious prize.
I hazard a guess upon their value.
What wealth to me those pearls had brought.

For oft upon the ocean I sail,
Tracing the Transatlantic trail.
They float upon the surface of my mind,
Which is a turbulent place to wander.
And then my soul in sad exile soars
And dances in the splendour of the sky.

Air Mail Letters

They called my great-granny Gerty "Pot Salt,"
Though she was kind and generous to fault.

She seasoned her sauces with sprigs of thyme,
Teaching children how to reason and rhyme.

One time she showed me how to peel onions,
Then used them to remedy her bunions.

She gave my granny Ida a basket of ginger
To ease the pain in her inflamed big finger.

She cured my cough with cloves of garlic,
Saying a kitchen was no place for a girl-child to frolic.

She used to grow Scotch bonnet peppers,
And posted dried seeds to me in Air Mail letters.

Space Invader: Ode to Star Trek

I used to think you were a shooting star,
Hurtling through space at the speed of light,
Heading this way on a collision course,
Sinking into the dust of the African desert.

I used to think you were from outer space,
Blasting off in orbit like a rocket man,
Flaming in the sky like a new-born star,
Circling my planet like an orbiting black hole.

I used to think the world was round,
Spinning on its axis like a wooden top,
Rotating on Atlas' finger-tip,
Yet standing still at the stroke of midnight.

I used to think we were binary stars,
Speeding towards earth like Haley's Comet,
Exploding in space like a meteorite storm,
Showering the world with our cosmic dust.

I even used to think stars, comets and meteors
Were God's naughty children seen in the sky,
God stomping his right foot at them in a rage,
Causing thunder to roll and lightning to strike.

But now, I know, you're a space invader.

The Reaper's Garden

"My hair is distinctly bespoke – like my outfits."
Not unlike unread books, Dee sat on the shelf
Vaping and sending out weekly smoke signals.
"I paid for it, so it's mine – real Brazilian hair."

"It is what it is. Mine is Asian – good quality."
Beady-eyed Bee studied the competition:
Besties blending in with the loud sound system.
"Afros and perms are too high maintenance."

"Bye-bye to pink sponge rollers and hot combs!"
Coal black hair extensions had transformed Tee.
Elbowed aside, braids were fast disappearing,
Though weaves and wavy wigs owned the room.

"Me, going natural? What! Afro-pussy?"
Trying to hazard a guess who fell within
Certain hair textures seemed pointless to Cee,
What with the talk turning to shaving below.

"It's like an annual Afghan dog show in here."
Heels hit the floor to *Who Let the Dogs Out?*
Golden crown of curls framed egg-shell white faces,
Tethering the black bulls among the cow herd.

"Whoa! What! Me, take my natural hair to work?"
Managing stigmatised identities on the dancefloor,
Shaking off rejection by the future "seed sowers"
And those who would tend the reaper's garden.

Foodies: Colour Coding

"I need to get myself in the ball game too."
Dressed in black lycra leggings and a blue top,
The baby mother pushed a new stroller.
"I gotta get rid of this donkey booty."
"Our old folks didn't diet – cotton picking."
Vee was always counting the calories
And had taken to colour coding food.
"I feel like I age waiting for opportunity…"

"Tell me about it." Lycra leggings considered.
"Southern men like big donkey booties."
She parked her stroller and did some stretches,
Repeating, "Eat less and exercise more."

    Like a child having a tantrum outdoors,
    Vee wheeled off. "I'm not ditching the beige."

Terra Firma

"Choose your clothes with dress code in mind."
Jess Van Dijk slipped into an aged fox fur coat,
Engaging in her usual dressing up.
"A well-made outfit will always stand out."

"The wrong uniform could spell disaster,"
She said. "No recognition at all."
Caressing the old fox fur, she sighed,
"Lose the Afro, dear; it's too militant."

"The first question should always begin:
What is the dress code for this position?"
She slipped out of the Seventies coat.
"Court shoes, navy tights and a woollen suit."

"Afros are so passé – Angela Davis."
She raked over the old travelling trunk,
Fishing out a man's velvet smoking jacket.
"I love men in thick cord trousers and…"

"I see you with a vagabond bad boy, dear."
A widow and former costume designer,
Jess was trapped in a long gone time and place.
"Aw shucks! My Father's Knickerbocker outfit."

"You were asking about my girlfriends earlier."
The locum carer jumped into the brief pause,
Inspecting a box of costume jewellery.
"All my friends are single – soccer mommas."

"Your men should wear bullet proof vests, honey."
In her daydreaming hours, dark masses
Clustered together like even-toed cattle.
"Stags competing for mating rights to white…"

"I need a vacation, somewhere exotic."
It would take another century to shift
The biases implanted by history.
"I'd love a cruise. I hate water – *terra firma*."

The Yellow Butterfly

She left her child-bed on the third day,
Walking slowly out into the fresh air,
And as she was studying a butterfly,
A gust of wind dashed it from the porch.

Not long after, the butterfly was back:
Yellow, with broken wings, still struggling.
This time, it landed on the manicured lawn,
Losing its very reason to exist.

As she was bending to inspect it,
A black veiny hand fell on her shoulder
(Resembling the withered wings of a ratbat),
Remarking that the clouds were hanging low.

Quite unexpectedly, a bird swooped down
And landed on the lawn in the sunshine
While an army of ants worked as a team.
The arm lifted like leaves swirling through the air.

Black Velvet

What can I say to make you feel better
About putting down your pampered setter?
Your brown eyes are full of remembrance,
Except that they've not seen much repentance.

I stopped pandering to your pet's demands,
Because it became too sulky with reprimands.
Its coat reminds me of smooth Black Velvet,
As if caressing a moth-eaten comfort blanket.

What can I do to make a stand?
Seeing that you still do not understand
That a dog is not really man's best friend,
Hoping you'll allow me to make amends.

> How you loved taking that pooch for walks,
> Watching her spinning and chasing her own tail.

Burning Spear: Ode to Robert Burns

My love is like a burning spear
That's newly forged in steel.
My love is like the birth pains
I feel that fill me up with real fear.

As dark art thou, my lover boy,
So deep with hate is my heart to aspire!
And I will hate you, massa-o, until the day you expire.
And I will hate you, massa-o, until the sea weeps with joy.

Till all the seas sink into the earth's core
And the winds of war blow you apart!
And I will hold my Nubian lover in my heart
Until the Rock of Gibraltar is no more.

And I will write a poem about a rose,
And I will scatter rosebuds without delay.
And I will mould my lover's face in clay,
As tho' he were sleeping in sweet repose.

The Squatters

They came out of a disused letter box,
Crawling under the "out of plane" front door;
Newly-hatched spiders learning with mother,
Heading straight for the fleapit sitting-room.

Standing sentry on the "Welcome" door mat,
A slow yawn escaped the resident cat,
Watching the procession in the hallway,
Following the clutter into the lounge.

Pressed by fatigue, the squatter sat down
To a plateful of homemade fish and chips,
Tossing a red snapper at the grey cat
Whose fur on his back stood up in alarm!

>The mouse trap's jaws shut in the far corner
>Where an old spider was spinning her web.

The Chameleon

The twilight began with a swishing sound,
Like a predator stalking in silence.
Blending in with the shades of the forest,
The chameleon climbed a cedar tree.

"I'm invisible." She looked around her.
Famed for her ability to change colour,
Altering her pigment to ward off threats,
She moved on top of the outer tree bark.

Rocking her long body between each step,
The chameleon aped a blowing leaf,
Rotating and focusing her eyes in unison,
As if they both moved independently.

Cunning, she blended into the background,
Tongue darting out at an alarming speed,
Catching a grass-hopper on its maiden flight
And chewing with her sharp, saw-like teeth.

Housemaid's Knee

Faye was on all fours polishing the floor,
Grumbling about avoiding housemaid's knee.
Bright eyed, her puppy came through the door,
Longing to say loudly, "I want to wee."

"What have you done?" Faye said aghast,
Dipping the wet sponge into the bucket.
"You little scamp. Good job the rug is colourfast.
Wagging your bushy tail just won't cut it."

"There's a ginger cat stuck up the oak tree."
Her man wiped his feet on the back doormat.
"You naughty boy. I see you've done a pee."
He heard meowing coming from the cat.

"You ought to rescue him: poor little Judd."
Faye stood up and called time on the job.
Outdoor, the stranded cat fell with a thud.
"I'm done with housework. Get a cleaner, Bob."

Dog Roses

We rose at dawn with anticipation
For the sow had been in labour all night.
Slipping out of the back door at first light,
We ran as though racing the forest fire.

The dog roses seemed displaced in the thickets
Where the ground doves were cooing clearly.
Shame-mi-lion[33] grass flattened beneath our feet,
As if they were hiding their nakedness from us.

Over the fence we leapt in high spirits,
Eager to see the new litter of pigs.
Thrilled, our small voices raised to crescendo:
"Black, brown, white – all from the same mother!"

Excited, we returned to the hall for breakfast.
The house mother's waters broke too soon for life.
It was a boy with a shock of black hair.
Suddenly, the weather turned quite stormy.

---

33. "Chameleon grass."

On the Brink

Pandas chewing on bamboo shoots in China.
Conservationists checking faeces in the wilds,
Seeking teeth marks to determine numbers:
Extinction status downgraded to vulnerable.

Born in captivity – enjoying a charmed existence,
Cameras capturing cuddly black-eyed babies
Suckling with their white faces and black ears
Under the adoring gaze of the watching world.

Passage to India, Royal Bengali tiger threatened.
Solitary by nature, stalking monkeys in Mumbai,
Birthing the next generation in five to six months,
Big cats hunted to the brink…in tropical rainforests.

Out of Africa and one step closer to extinction!
Sub-species of eastern gorillas under threat,
Prowling the lowlands and roaring in the mist,
Poaching adding to decline in their natural habitat.

Big man's meat on the menu for army big-wigs,
VIPs chomping on important man's bush meat
In the DRC and neighbouring lands,
Species uplisted as critically endangered.

Bellowing elephants stripping trees of bark,
Herds on the march across the open plains.
Bones piled high in Africa's graveyard,
Trophy hunting for ivory – highly prized in China.

Revels in Jamaica – a day at Hope Zoo,
Showcasing island's big lizards named iguana,
Hunted to near extinction by the introduction
Of nineteenth century Indian mongoose.

Rare boas on list in My Green Hills of Jamaica,
Bred in captivity and released into the wilds,
Protected by law yet destroyed by man's hand,
Habitat in rock crevasses and limestone caves.

Conservation landscapes across the globe!
Song birds warbling by nature under threat:
Wildpine Sergeat or the Jamaican Blackbird,
Their natural habitat in Mount Diablo.

The Fickle Weather

The stiff-haired sows roam the uplands,
Scavenging on decaying wasted matter;
Fattening up themselves for hungry times,
And making their way down to the lowlands.

The dry season comes with a violent thirst
In the dust-laden valley of cactus beds.
In the pastures, cattle graze on dry grass –
Near collapse, a bull stands with wooden tongue.

The seasonal rains are now a distant memory,
But the fickle weather takes a sudden turn.
After months of drought, expectations raised high,
Much, much higher than the Atlas Mountains.

When the warm rain rolls in on the thunder,
The wild sows descend on a cloudburst.
Searching for a new feeding trough,
They wallow in the muddy riverbed.

Watery Wealth

"I know this land better than anyone else,"
She said, being a good steward of the earth.
Had she not sown seeds of kindness often
And watered the arid land in times of drought?

"Our people cried until their tears formed a lake."
She pointed to a sheet of still water,
Extending a long slender finger.
"When it dries up, our tears will turn to salt."

"Our foremothers crafted shell necklaces!
They used eggshells as water containers, too."
She raised an axe, splitting a deadly snake,
Keeping great poise like an elegant egret.

> It had been hanging from a branch that morning,
> Waiting to drop on an unsuspecting walker.

The Water Carrier

Balancing the water pan on her head at dawn,
She had cushioned the weight with a *cotta*.[34]
A sigh escaped the forgotten woman's lips,
As she returned home from the public tank.

After a dry spell of almost twelve months,
She was forced to walk a mile to fetch water
For her cooking pot and the family's needs,
Even though she was nursing her fourth child.

When she had emptied the magical drops
Into the shipping barrel called "a drum",
She made a crackling fire with brushwood,
Staving off a swarm of tiny winged predators.

Drained, she washed and hung out the clothes to dry,
Then she proffered a full breast to her baby boy
(Keeping the biting insects away with a fly swat),
While the morning sun crept through the branches.

---

34. This refers to a long piece of fabric that is then shaped like a doughnut and placed on a person's head to balance loads such as a bundle of wood or a bucket of water.

The Dance of the Snakes

She had an innate need to express herself,
Talking constantly at public events,
Outdoing the chattering parakeets,
Sounding rather like a broken record.

There was also the temptation to share all
On social media by posting photos
And entertaining her global friends
With gossip and her "woe is me" stories.

"Why don't you talk to your work mates, Mel,
Even if it's about the price of fish?"
The sister with the puff-ball hair-style asked,
Probing her colleague's mind to find the fear.

"Have you thought of wearing control girdles, Mel?
Spandex is kind to stomachs and wobbly bits."
The puff-ball sister was a Facebook friend,
Who posted video clips on Mel's website.

"Take a look," said Mel. "The dance of the snakes."
Legless danger lurked in the undergrowth:
The male grabbed his lover behind her neck,
Dry biting, though not flooding her with venom.

"You crazy woman." Puff-ball was speechless.
Having entwined their necks ungraciously,
The snakes locked together in their love dance.
"I'm not putting that on my Facebook page, Mel."

"Sometimes they lay like that for days or weeks."
The unfriending phase began with the grim
Theatricality of the snake dance.
"They're having a hoot – not quite a leg over."

The Crossing

They walked this roadway in ages past,
Wedges of wild swans waddling with wildings,
Protected by the crown and claiming right of way,
Risking lives to reach water on the Thames tributaries!
Commoners committing crime poaching "special status" swans,
Respected and reserved for the dinner plates of noblemen.

Spring dances with dew-bedecked daffodils on the downs,
Signalling the arrival of Easter dressed up in her bonnet.
A murder of crows roost in a tree under the stalking moon.
Birds of a feather dream of decomposing banqueting dish,
Regurgitating images of road-killed animals: "Carrion comfort."

Summer arrives on waterways and in urban wetlands.
Season after season swans fly over in a v-shaped formation!
Hissing, Mama Pen glides along a dual carriageway,
Five cygnets in single file with Papa Cob leading the clutch.
Unmarked and unaware of the annual "swan-upping" on the Thames:
Scarlet blazers, brass buttons and rowing skiffs with flying flags.

Flared wings! Flighty cygnet in the path of oncoming traffic.
Juddering juggernaut flattens a mass of maternal white feathers!
Commuters' cameras flash in a forest lost in the mist of time.
Jogging Jeremiah jests about swans "in a coffin of rye paste."
Horns honking, hurling expletives ("Effing swanning about"),
Putting the motherless cygnets more and more on edge.

Another day and the family must brave the crossing again:
"Mission survive!" Papa Cob marshals cygnets across junction.
As summer wanes, he sails on water like Drake's Golden Hind.
Brooding, he grunts at bowing swans entwining long necks,
Expressing his natural reaction to their tedious courtship rituals.
Swanning off, he dips his head below water, never to mate again.

Selfie With Nye Bevan

In Cardiff city there stands a statue
Commemorating Aneurin Bevan,
Perched on his stout plinth to rival Churchill
And fixed in the Welsh nation's memory.

A far cry from mining in the valleys,
Belting out Baptist and Methodist hymns:
Eloquent orator, miner, left-winger
And famed Union leader from the Ebbw Vale.

The Labour Party's most lionised son,
Cast in bronze to honour the great Welshman,
Claiming his own place in British history
As founder of the National Health Service.

A heavyweight in the political arena,
Bevan could not have foreseen today's dispute:
Junior doctors forced to take strike action,
Waving militant placards: "Save our NHS!"

I Wonder Why: Ode to Jeannie Kirby

I wonder why the moon is white and round
And why the world spins around?

Who taught the birds and bees to fly
And told all the nations to go multiply?

O, when my big black bear just won't bellow,
Where can I find one that's not so yellow?

Who parted the clouds so the sky could weep
And gave the foxes a hole to sleep?

Who made the blue ocean so wide
And commanded the red sea to divide?

Why is it so, my nice neighbours decide,
That they won't allow "darkies" to reside?

The Colon-Man: Ode to The Pedlar's Caravan

I wish I lived in a canvas tent,
With a donkey-cart to drive like a Colon-Man!
Where he hails from, nobody knows,
Or where he camps in the evening dusk.

His canvas tent has a slit for a door
And a space within where he lays his head.
He has a brown woman and a baby girl,
And they go trotting from town to country!

"Any ole iron to repair, an' pots to weld?"
She clashes her cymbals like two brass plates.
Pots, pans and irons she carries in the cart,
Making a mobile home for her man and child.

The roads are rough and the lanes are grassy,
But her home is just like a camping tent.
The child, she likes to play with her air friends,
Skipping and larking on the mountainside.

With the Colon-man I would like to learn,
To read and write Spanish on my travels.
All the people would read my Spanish tales,
Just like *The Adventures of Don Quixote!*

Saturday's Child

"Now is di 'arvest – di time of reapin'."
Four elders sat beneath a guava tree,
Stuffing tobacco leaves into clay pipes,
Burning cow dung to keep the insects at bay.

"How yuh an' di back pain keepin', Pu-tus?"
Miss Zulie, the midwife, was in attendance:
Stoking the slumbering embers in the stove,
Boiling a selection of herbs for an enema.

"Di chile comin' a long way." Heads nodded,
Gazing at a lizard in the June flower tree.
Blowing his throat out like an orange balloon,
It watched a hummingbird, nectar dipping.

"If I lose dis chile, I gwine ban mi belly an' bawl.
Mi womb drop dung afta di las' miscarriage."
Thick black clouds had hid the moon all night.
The expectant mother was anxious to give birth.

At the appointed hour, the "canal" opened.
Every shade of bile had marred the pregnancy.
Miss Zulie had rubbed the stomach with aloe vera,
Carefully massaging the large navel.

"Learn yer lesson – learn it well, baby-gal."
The rain sealed her arrival with thunderclaps.
Lightning struck a fig tree to sounds of wailing.
"Di path of yer people stretch long behind yuh."

"Di song seh 'fus a gal an' second a bwoy'."
Cutting the cord, the smiling midwife stopped
To look at a visitor hanging from the ceiling:
"Welcome, Wise One – di Great Spider."

Jippy-Jappa Hat

Shoes slung over shoulder with knotted laces,
Day-dreaming of china dolls without faces;
Snoozing on sand with sunbeams shining down.

Jippy-jappa[35] hat shielding head by the seashore,
Memories of elegant waterfowls gliding on a lakeshore;
Drowning man clutching at straws in-between screams.

Stunned sisters building sandcastles on the beach,
Granny explaining that the man was beyond reach;
Death marring happy sandcastle-making afternoon.

---

35. "Straw hat."

Fire Sparkle

Was it my other self I dreamed of, Ama:
The girl with full eyes and fat plaits?
Or did I dream of a small spirit child,
Trying to lure my mini me away?

I lay on my bed dreaming of you, Ama:
The "wire-waist" girl with a hula hoop,
Swinging her hips like a half-grown woman,
Toying with a candy-striped rubber ring.

My memories hold black and white snapshots:
Headmaster, Teacher Llewelyn, in glasses!
And green uniform girls listening to his story
Of Gelert, the faithful Welsh hound.

My head houses questions and answers:
A fleeting scene in Kellits on Grand Market Day.[36]
"What do your eyes, likkle girl?"[37] the man asked.
"Fire sparkle burn me sir," she replied.

My eyelids flicker with the painful memories:
Ah! Coloured light bulbs thronging the streets,
Higglers in plaid headties weighing mangoes;
Children blowing *fee-fees*[38] and big balloons.

Other scenes float on a raft in my mind, too:
Morning mist on a carpet of long-bladed grass,
Mockingbirds bringing the hills alive with sound;
Roosters brawling with assertive flip of wings.

I dreamed once that I saw Aladdin's Cave,
Stuffed to the rafters with precious stones.
But I was not tempted by the treasures –
A jewelled-eyed serpent guarded the entrance.

---

36. This is the traditional Christmas Eve market day in Jamaica.
37. "What is wrong with your eyes, little girl?"
38. "A whistle."

The Hills of Zion: Ode to Charles Kingsley

Oh, Martha, go and bring the goats home,
And bring the goats home,
And bring the goats home,
Across the hills of Zion!

The evening sun went down with the rain,
And off she went in a roll of thunder.

The hurricane winds whipped up over the hills,
And o'er and o'er the hills,
And round and round the hills,
As far as sound could travel.

The rain came down with a rising fog,
And never home came Martha!

Oh! Is it rags, or scarf, or a headtie,
A square of calico cloth,
A broken body impaled
On the sharp pointed rocks?
Was never crayfish swam so fast
Among the shrimps in the roaring river.

They carried her across the jagged rocks,
The precipitous Cockpit Mountain range,
The open jaws of the ancient valley,
To her resting place beside the bamboo trees.
But still the locals hear her calling the goats home,
Across the hills of Zion.

The Collectors of Souls

"Come away, come away," the night spoke in whispers.
"Will you not come away?" the voices coaxed.
"Come away from that empty, arid place,"
Urged the collectors in their soft voices.

Black robes draped over their stick-thin shoulders.
Skin withered away with protruding ribs,
And sunken eyes filled with a thousand lives!
"Come away from that desolate ruin."

In spite of the sun and the raging heat,
Blind boys built jet-black sand cathedrals,
While girls, uncovered from the waist up,
Sat on the sand, singing, "Skip, skip, skip to my lou…"

> "Come away from there. Come, give up the fight.
> Come, sleep away the dark night of the soul."

The Flame Tree: Ode to Thomas Hood

I recall, I recall,
The place where I was raised:
The green grass where the moon
Cast her shadow on the lawn.
She never left before approaching dawn,
Nor brought too short a night.
But now, I often wish her beams
Would not creep into my dreams.

I recall, I recall,
The poincianas, orange and red,
The hibiscuses, red, yellow and white:
Those showy flowers with deep green leaves!
The bromeliads growing wild on branches,
And where my granny planted
The flame tree on my flight-day:
The blood-red flowers cover the ground still.

I recall, I recall,
When I used to pour indigo into the river,
And thought that I could wash the blue out of the sea.
My imagination soared on wings then
That have been clipped now.
But all the mean and ugly years could not douse
The fire of ambition burning in my veins.

I recall, I recall,
The silk cotton tree, tall and stout.
I thought the trunk could reach the sky.
It was a childish thought, reaching for the sky,
But now there's so much joy
To know I am nearer to my goal
Than when I was a girl.

The Mentor

She resembled an anorexic bird,
Lying on her feather-stuffed sofa,
Knowing she could not afford to be nice
And sensing my disillusion with her.

She insisted on being a critical friend:
Tricking her way into folk's confidence,
Planting the seed of doubt on fertile soil,
Watching their hand-wringing with disdain.

A woman who appreciated quality
Rather than quantity and imperfection,
She regarded herself as today's front page,
Insisting tomorrow was for stale news.

She had that certain something about her
That separated her from the common folk,
Often polishing their tarnished stars,
Whilst parcelling out blame and praise.

Comfort: On the Death of a Neighbour's Daughter (1982)

Black, pink and white clouds marred the night sky.
The father leaned on yesterday's broken fence,
The smell of his daughter's perfume (Charlie)
Lingering on the air like burnt incense.

Distraught, his wife tore at her clothes and hair,
While the neighbours waited with bated breaths.
He saw the flames in his wife's eyes – clear pools,
Eye-water sprouting out with every scream.

The smell of smoke and sooty phlegm in her throat,
Oiling her tonsils and filling her lungs:
Comfort did her homework by candlelight;
A breath of wind fanned the flames on the roof.

>   Six firemen walked through the human wreckage,
>   Gazing solemnly at the burnt remains.

Comfort: The Vigil

Her soul drifted upwards on the black smoke.
Her real crime, by a cruel trick of fate,
Had been to revise by the light of wax:
The candle fell over and the fire raged.

All night her parents sat in the ashes,
Counting the cost of hazard fire candles,
Keeping the vigil in the smoke-scented house,
Nostrils filled with the scent of burning foam.

They gave her up on a wet soggy day.
The usual crowd came to pay their respects,
Though not the reserved flushed-faced white neighbours
Who watched the cortege from behind curtains.

> The grieving mother's friends cooked jolof rice:
> "You have a direct line to the ancestors now."

Garden Statuary

Garden statuary was their passion.
They had a host of weathered stone gnomes,
Which created a focal point in the borders,
Some looking as if they were leprechauns.

Hidden among the blackberry borders
Were the stately-looking or grotesques faces
Of statues cast in Victorian times:
Pixies, lions, gargoyles and the Four Seasons.[39]

"I can't be doing with peacocks, but busts…"
A smile grew on the head gardener's face.
"Oh lordy! They're easier on the eye."
He took a step back, studying the Three Graces.[40]

"*Ooh arr*! I wouldn't mind a wee slice of *tharr.*"
The keen-eyed under-gardener grinned,
Bending to inspect a fleshy stone rear.
Green fingered aspirations climaxed with a gasp.

---

39. Greco-Roman goddesses of the seasons.
40. Neoclassical sculpture of the mythological three charities or daughters of Zeus: Euphrosyne, Aglaia and Thalia.

Kerosene Light

Last night, I read by kerosene light,
Leaving a blue bookmark to remind me
Where I stopped before my lamp-wick burnt low
In the study where I returned the next day.
Someone had been reading my borrowed book!
The marker was not where I had left it.
Pages were creased, torn and even dog-eared.
The book was read from cover and cover.
It was highlighted and marred in the margins,
But there was no one around except me.
The windows and door were tightly shut, too!
Who had vandalised my revision book?

>   I was reminded of the dream-walker:
>   My alter ego, KEE, was a night reader.

Celebrity Fridge

Attached to the new double-front fridge
Was a magnet: "Too blessed to be stressed."
In the freezer, she placed a leg of lamb,
A shoulder of pork and a pound of beef.

In the bottom compartment was ham hock,
A side of bacon and some frozen fish.
Below this she kept frozen peas in pods,
And a selection of bread and ice-cream.

Into the main fridge she placed perishables,
Such as eggs, milk, cheese, butter and yoghurt.
Inside the fridge door she stored beverages,
Like water, mango and passion fruit juice.

On the top rack she kept wine and champagne
For that special day and anniversaries,
Selecting the sweet white wines for birthdays,
And Crystal champagne for her achievements.

There was a cooler for fresh vegetables,
And space for sauces, cream cakes and iced-tea.
She was too organised "to be stressed,"
What with having a celebrity fridge!

Voices

They fill my head with their mental chatter:
Disembodied voices with no flesh on bones,
Disturbing the peace in my quiet bed,
Squandering my time with their empty words.

They stuff my head with trivial matter:
Monotonous voices with their flat tones,
Chipping away at my mind in the dark,
Telling me my face doesn't fit the profile.

They cram my head with small talk to flatter:
Calm voices that break the ugly silence,
Judging me by my faults and failures,
Pointing to my disappointments and my strife.

They crowd my head with their constant natter:
Crowing voices that shatter my eardrums,
Some cackling like hens in my solitude,
Teetering on the edge of falling asleep.

Taking Words Apart

If you asked about my hobbies, I'd say:
I enjoy reading and writing stories.
I also like "gathering nuts in May."
And when I get the time, I bake cookies.

O yes, and I like taking words apart!
Often rearranging my study room,
Finding place to put my art for a start,
And sweeping the house with my bamboo broom.

Then again, I like viewing historic places,
Taking photos of hiking adventures,
Visiting friends and seeing new faces,
And participating in joint ventures.

Of course, I like to entertain at home,
Eat and drink with long lost family members.
Not to mention my frequent flights to Rome,
And stoking a fire with glowing embers.

Block Capitals

People say I'm simple, gentle and weak.
Perhaps. I really can't argue with them.
What I do know is that I have foresight,
And I don't give my foes a second chance.

I love to string words like a daisy chain,
Placing them in alphabetical order
To make them appear like a garland,
Or even a group of beads on a frame.

If I'm weak, it is a weakness for "winners,"
Though I do go weak at a drop of blood,
And weak-kneed at the sight of a six pack!
Oh, I'm a sucker for a slice of cake.

Gentle is a word I use to stoke fires,
Tossing Simple Simon in the fireplace.
I take words with spoons of cod liver oil,
Passing the Block Capitals in my stools.

A Garland of Words

A story is told with a garland of words,
Using imagination, assonance,
Imagery, alliteration, pauses, metaphors,
A shared culture, personification,
Private and personal experiences.
Words are sometimes not enough to say it:
To describe the forest from the dense woods
In one go, using sand and building blocks.
A story can be classed as orature:
The story-teller sits and tells a tale,
Acting as repository of knowledge,
Passing on myths and legends to others.

> But most of all, a good story should have
> A beginning, middle and a sharp end.

Some People

Some people spend their whole lives
Waiting for the right one to come along;
Others fritter away valuable time,
Asking, "What if tomorrow never comes?"

Some people make much ado about nothing.
Musical people sit "on the dock of the bay."
Righteous people kneel at the altar and pray.
Lively people "get down" and party all day.

Those same people weep at the loss of a pet,
Turning their stony gazes the other way
At the sight of a vagrant in distress.
Yet they drink the wine of absolution on Sundays.

     Negative people drink "the cup of bitterness";
     Top people drink 'til "their cup runneth over."

The Eye of the Egg

Inside the shell of an egg
There's a yoke that's yellow,
Rich in nutrients
And surrounded by a white fluid,
Which, when boiled, hardens like a sponge ball.
Fast asleep within the yoke,
Growing undisturbed without light in the dark,
There's an eye that cannot see,
But it feeds off the nutrients
Until it grows into a chicklet.
"Wake," says the sunlight,
"Come and take flight!"

    And the featherless egg-crusted chicklet
    Breaks out, only to hide under its mother's wings.

Gourd Tree: Ode to the Little Nut Tree

I have an ancient gourd tree in my yard.
Nothing will it yield but big white berries
And a golden bough with reddish-brown leaves
That turn to yellow and green in winter.
The King of Dahomey's kidnapped daughter
Came to visit back in the eighteenth century,
All because of that hosting gourd tree.
The centuries have flown by like flying birds
And clinging vines have weakened the tree,
Which has seen generations come and go!
Each Christmas it shows off its mistletoes
Whose bearer draws nutrient from its host.

> I would not cut that parasitic vine
> For it brings smiles under the mistletoe.

The Good Samaritan

Exhausted and thirsty on the hard shoulder,
Running out of petrol on my lonesome.
Glad I felt when a rescue lorry stopped,
Offering me a lift to the nearest petrol station.

"A kind act won't put me out of my way,"
He said, heading for the service station,
With his foghorn blaring in the bright lights,
Proffering a half-flask of luke-warm tea.

Two lorries pulled out of the petrol station,
One turning left in the direction of Kent;
The other speeding towards South London.
None had stopped to assist her earlier.

Too busy chatting on their mobile phones,
Too late to apply emergency brakes!
The crushed cyclist lay trapped under a wheel:
Two lorry-drivers in a state of shock.

Like a regular jolly jack-in-the-box,
The Good Samaritan popped up again.
"There's not much we can do for the lad, Miss.
I'd better see you safely back to your car."

Pink Bus to Battersea (2015)

"Man-hater!" The lone wolf's voice raised the roof
Of the New Addington Community Hall.
A one-man band waving his protest placard.
"Don't believe a word! She's a man-hater!"

Local women had come out to meet and greet
The Pink Bus Brigade outside the hall
In one of the most deprived Croydon wards,
A stone's throw from the wealthy West Purley.

"Sorry, Harriet (Harman). I can't support Labour
If you can't take a photograph with me."
Pink rose quartz necklace and matching earrings
Complemented her crisp pink cotton shirt.

The local candidates reeled off their words,
Leaving no room for a foot-in-mouth moment,
Or even a quick Q & A session!
Off the pink bus trundled to Battersea.

Digging Up the Past: Independence Day

The long years have left their scars on my mind,
But none more so than nineteen sixty-two!
Of this, I am definitely certain.
When back I came on Independence Day
With dashed hopes of special edition plate,
Or perhaps even a souvenir mug.
That was the day I experienced fear:
Someone choked on a paradise plum sweet!
The adults denied us our mementos,
For they were not future thinking people.
On the night after Independence Day,
We sat up until the morning stars faded.

> Then we hoisted our green, black and gold flag!
> Digging up the past: "Jamaica, Land We Love."

Easter Monday

In the Motherland on Easter Monday,
Setting an egg in a glass of water
Was one way of predicting the future.
First, place egg white in a glass of water
Before the sun shows up on Good Friday.
When the sun rises on Good Friday morn,
A pattern is formed by the egg white.
For example, a gallows means "hang 'em high";
A ship indicates that you will travel;
A ring symbolises that you will marry;
An aircraft means you will travel by air.
Of course, a coffin means a death to come!
If all these future predictions scare you,

> There is always kite sailing on Easter Monday,
> And spiced bun and cheese to sweeten the day.

Our Coat of Arms

Black blood soaking the earth like pitch lake.
"Clean country" gorging on "dead carrion."
Pulling foot with pounding hearts in mouths:
Stateless and in a constant state of flight!

"Wooeeee!" Men playing dominoes on shop piazza.
Parson drinking mannish water in dead yard.
Barefoot children climbing Blue Mahoe trees.
Coconut in rice an' peas on Sundays.

Crocodile cruising Alligator Pond.
Doctor-bird nesting on Anancy's web.
Galliwasp endangered by India's mongoose.
White *sense*[41] fowl spinning in the *balmyard*![42]

Earth man chanting Babylon down, down!
Reggae singers in red, green and gold tams.
Drums beating out national heroes names:
"Cudjoe, Nanny, Tacky, Sharpe, Bogle, Gordon..."

Keeping up our Easter traditions:
Setting egg white in water to see the future,
Cutting the bleeding nut tree on Good Friday;
Sailing multi-coloured kites Easter Monday!

Cooking ackee an' salt fish in Dutch pot,
Reciting the National Pledge "by heart."
Singing National Anthem Independence Day,
Arawaks and pineapples on our Coat of Arms.

---

41. This is a chicken with sparse, uneven and ruffled feathers, often used in rituals as a sacrifice.
42. A place where healing rituals are performed.

Yabba Pot: The Good Old Days

What happened to the days when our women
Carried grip baskets at their sides in the hills
Where farmers planted *Gros Michel* bananas,
And gave each other a day's work in lieu?

Ah, the good old days when "the love" flowed from
A tight-knit community of "skin colour."
True, teeth and tongue courted old time sayings:
"Yuh mout' big like yabba pot, 'urry com' up."

What happened to the days of "ground-clothes,"
When farm-working men took sides in disputes,
Wielding sharp machetes and blustering?
"Unu 'old me back 'fore mi chop up 'im *warra-warra!*"[43]

Back then, babies' heads crowned after long hours
Squatting on chamber-pots and coir mattresses,
And old folks "gave up the ghost" in the arms
Of their loved ones: "Rock of ages cleft for me…"

What happened to the days when labouring men
(Parochial road workers) dug up a song?
"*K'lamie*[44] tek out 'im big white sheet wid all di rice
An' curry goat meat, an' all di *jankro* cum dung fi eat…"

Loose limbed limbo dancers livened up a wake,
Killing the quadrille under the fire stick!
Hips moving in rhythm to the beat of drums,
Going down with thighs spread wide as the ocean.

What happened to the days when the parson
Railed against bongo drums and the vulgar body?
Oh, and sly mothers-in-law winked with the eye:
"Whai-o! Du son, nuh giv' 'er nuh more licks!"

---

43. Often said in anger to avoid using expletives, especially words for private parts.
44. A traditional healer or *"Obeahman."*

In-between the *su-su-suing*[45] about
Bredda Hog rooting Maas Pepe's wife's ground,
Tongues engaged in peppery exchanges:
"Fas' mout' dead an' gone; bitter belly lef' ya."

What happened to the days when children
Enjoyed the simple pleasure of seeing
Twin *guineps*[46] in the green shell of childhood,
Playing cricket in the schoolyard at break?

---

45. Derogatory word for women whispering.
46. A small green fruit which has a jelly-like pulp that contains a large seed.

Forget-Me-Not

The time of the traditional Kitchen Bitch[47]
Has passed into history with our foremothers,
Some still rising with the dead on rest days,
Chanting: "Kumbaya, lawd, kumbaya…"

Men pouring their life's blood into the land.
Women labouring in palatial splendour.
The enslaved hefting cast-iron pots off the fire,
Scorching their blue-black skin in the furnace.

Cotton trees standing silent in banana groves!
Sweet peas blooming out of cracks in the rocks.
A cruel beauty seen at the crack of dawn:
The hills coming alive with singing: "Kumbaya…"

Underwater springs bubbling up by the roadside.
Reed bed floating on top of pond-water.
Big lumps of red meat grazing in the pastures.
Washerwomen scrubbing little massa's drawers.

No proper public apology or reparations
For the hands that rocked the colonial cradles.
Ghostly dark shrunken eyes of forget-me-not,
Subsumed in a legal limbo: "Oh lawd, kumbaya…"

---

47. A small oil lamp used by the poor in colonial Jamaica.

Jamaican Talls

It was not always so with the coconut
Trees littering the countryside and our yard,
Providing a safe haven for green lizards
Jumping from limb to limb and lazing around.

Like their foreign counterparts, the black crows
(With their white necks resembling country parsons)
Ruled the roosts from the top of the coconut trees,
Swooping to snatch up a plague of bull frogs.

Elevated on a plateau, a cluster of trees
Had once been home to our coconut grove
Where woodpeckers bored away at the trunks,
While *jankros* gouged out the eyes of a dead cat.

To the local people the coconut trees
Were a part of the green landscape until a
Mystery disease killed the heads and spiny limbs:
Trees that reached a height of up to ten metres.

Years gone by, picking coconuts was
A daily task, using the flesh for cooking.
First, grate the hard white meat, then boil and skim,
Separating the "custard" from the oil.

Long before Western women discovered
Coconut as cooking oil and moisturiser,
Our women knew its value to oil their skin,
Make floor brushes, brooms, mats, hats and bags.

The Jamaican Talls stood in sepia photos,
Used for rice an' peas, drops, gizzadas, milk,
Run-down and fronds for roofing, jelly for children,
And shells for utensils and ornaments.

Tall and naked, they resemble giant posts!
Before anyone noticed that "the yellowing"
Disease was ravaging the island's coconut trees,
They had lost their spreading limbs – green boughs.

Compulsive Walkers

In the heart of the country of brushwood,
The dew-water lay still on the rosebuds,
Dampening the blush-pink and red petals,
While a late star stalked the morning sky.

Those were the days of the mule and donkey,
Chewing grass along the ancient footways,
Following the footsteps of the Taino people,
Repeating Arawakan words: "*Yaya, wayaba…*"[48]

From the storehouse of the past we stole stories,
Slashing new paths through the vales of plenty,
Charting acres and acres of lush countryside,
Guided by lines of invisible energy beneath our feet.

We saw the Sixties through a gifted View-Master,
Walking a good many miles across hills and dales.
Striding along, we raided nature's medicine chest,
Gathering herbs, roots and tree bark to cure ailments.

Drinking the liquid of life from a clear mountain stream,
We observed the water washing over basalt rocks:
Compulsive walkers carving out our own pathway,
Ramblers reciting: "Lawyer, doctor, Syrian, chief…"[49]

---

48. This Arawakan word is part of the lost language of the Indigenous people of Jamaica, used here as an echo from the past.
49. A childhood rhyme recited in the playground in rural Jamaica. Children dreamed of positions of power and status based on class and race. For example, the Syrians were the business people in colonial Jamaica.

Black Loyalist Beggars

Man snoozing on the heath without his chains,
Snuggled up in the eiderdown of dreams.
Another floating over lantern-lit Vauxhall Gardens,
Hearing the rattle of the night soil carts.

Daylight and sunrays on old Father Thames.
Frozen ice drifting like lumps of bread on water.
Day dawning to see soup kitchen Irish eyes,
Doling out mugs of thin gruel with stale rolls.

Black Loyalists dressed in tattered uniform in boat,
Looking as if they forgot to put their teeth in.
Montage of revolution going through their heads.
Drifters with chain scarred ankles: "Run, *naga*, run!"

> Northern girls linking iron chains to make a living,
> Chains rattling down time in the Black Country.[50]

---

50. The Black Country includes Wolverhampton, Dudley and Sandwell. Towns such as Cradley Heath, Old Hill, Quarry Bank and Netherton had a monopoly on chain making during the period of slavery.

The Archway of No Return

Meeting death ungallantly, leaping off rocks
At Desperation Point with chains on feet.
Fractured and restrained in another place,
Lives shackled by the winds of change.

Innocents entering the archway of no return,
Stolen or tricked away from their compounds.
Unpaid labour transported to another world.
Dead eyes looking beyond the horizon.

Though the strong had a faint glimmer of hope
On the epic journey to a life of toil and death,
The incessant cries and noises filled the hull
Ankle deep in bilge water in the stifling heat.

The sick and weak tossed overboard on the Zong,[51]
Substantial supper for the sharks in the sea:
Cavernous jaws with enormous sponge tongues,
Thrashing about in the aquamarine water.

Sleeping erratically in the dark pit of hell,
The children dreamed of skeletons in their beds.
Weeks ago, they were flesh and blood children:
Play disappeared with their stolen childhoods.

Forced to adapt to their new surroundings,
Wild-eyed souls stood ankle deep in corpses.
Minds muddled, succumbing to melancholy,
Locked in a dark place – robbed of humanity.

Stories passed from generation to generation
(Aches increasing with age and over-work),
Abducted and replanted against their will:
Human emotions beaten out with *cat-o-nine*.

---

51. J. Walvin, *The Zong: A Massacre, the Law and the End of Slavery* (New Haven: Yale University Press, 2011).

Walk-foot *backras* with predatory instincts,
Seeking their fortunes in the colonies.
Brutal natures drowning in guinea gold
Owning the four seasons of a man's life.

Pious men bending "the knee of righteousness."
Bystanders shrinking from denouncing the trade.
The weight of blackness burdened by racial bias:
A stumbling block in the path of future generations!

The Imperialist Yoke

Feeling the touch of an intrepid ancestor:
Freshwater African enduring the terror of travel,
Subjected to torture and humiliation *en-route*,
Seasoned and hiding himself in the grotto.

Senseless journeying dreams of savannahs,
Hunting big cats and celebrating with palm wine.
Dispossessed rebel with no place to call home:
Shelter-stone providing a refuge for this runaway.

One step closer to unchaining the chained one.
Captive thrilled to be free of the imperialist yoke!
Compensation settled on the owners of chattel,
Living in Wealthy Row dressed in their best tweed.

Wet cold spring with hard frost and rain at home,
Summer flowers adding colour to the landscape.
Autumn turning to winter in the Mother Country,
Icing over the trees in the uplands and lowlands.

"Tally-oh!" Riding out with a pack of barking hounds.
Fox hunting and quaffing champagne in the shires!
Stately piles with peacocking and preening on lawns,
Dressing the grouse meat for the lunchtime menu.

Returning to the great Caledonian pine forests,
Scots braving the gales of the passing seasons.
Folk diving into Loch Lomond fully clothed,
Suited and booted and enjoying pride of race.

Enemies of the Empire

Beyond the boundaries of the sugar fields,
Cane-cutters slept standing on their feet:
Lives fraught with the ever threat of the lash,
Linked together by race and colour coding.

Kwa stretched out inert like a slim black snake,
Mouth frothing with physical exhaustion on the run.
Tales of trials and tribulation written in his face,
Nursing a sabre wound above his left eye.

Runaways dreaming of a world to roam free,
Driven to the brink by the grave-diggers of Empire,
Wading through water in dense network of caves,
From whence Britannia could not rule the bushes.

Unbroken men defending their flanks in the hills:
The strongholds of resistance on bare foot,
Maroons, known as "the point of the spear."
Kwa, man of mettle, named himself "the shaft."

Kofi caught by pack hounds with dripping fangs,
Frosting eyes and festering sores on his feet,
Dawning realisation of another displacement,
Firing reels of spit in his master's face!

Maroons banished and deported to Canada,
Walking on the rock-hard ice in Nova Scotia.
Some sitting out winter in a cold climate,
Toned warriors diminished to a sack of bones.

Enemies of the Empire *en-route* to Free Town,
Sailing on ice breaking up in the sea of life,
Witnesses to black misery in the Emerald Isle,
Scarred by memories of another time and place.

Black Loyalist beggars removed from the realm.
Racial cleansing on Georgian England's streets,
Wiping their lives completely off the slate,
Writing back: *Our Children Free and Happy*.[52]

---

52. C. Fyfe (editor), *Our Children Free and Happy* (Edinburgh University Press, 1992).

Calico Petticoat Rebellion

At the start of a busy day in the great house,
Windows were flung open to cool the ladies.
Languid pink bodies lay on posted beds
Like cherished eggs in a nest of eider ducks.

Outwardly rebellious, the female cane-hands
Had taken the lead in the fight for freedom.
It gave no pleasure to see sisters licking stone,
Or men chained to carts with heaps of cut grass.

Kissing the statue's stone lips as if it were flesh,
Two house-girls were feeling female power.
They'd refused to empty the ladies' night soil,
Causing the mistress to bring them to heel.

Helping to take the statue down off her perch,
A key driver in this calico petticoat rebellion
Was a "seasoned Negro" renamed Aura,
Derided for having "the sootiest complexion."

Swinging their pendulous breasts in history's face
(Milk leaking like the livestock on the plantation),
The rebels dumped the statue in an algae pond,
Humanising themselves by discussing their children.

The simmering feud between master and slaves
Relayed a message to their tyrannical owner
(Laying claim to their bodies and their children)
That they would not sink in a stagnant pool of self-pity.

They had knocked Helen of Troy off her perch.
Beaming modestly, the beguiling stone lady
Lay in shallow water surrounded by lilies
Like a pearl trapped in fossilised cow dung.

Retracing her steps back to ancient Greece
Was not an option for this pillar of virtue,
Whose alabaster skin was carved out of marble,
And adorned with a classic white toga.

Exquisite wild flowers grew near the pond.
Here men who put their wealth in black ivory
Reduced underage workhands to near paralysis:
Potters pressing their fingers into soft clay.

"Sugar!" The sound of a donkey braying indoors.
Wheel turning and a great flurry of activity!
Exchanging pleasantries over an impromptu visit.
Netted white faces heating up dramatically in the mill.

Merchant City

I have an oak writing desk from the seventeenth century,
And female journals rescued from the dustbin of history.
You see my face lined like the map of Merchant City,
But you cannot see the missing faces in my brown eyes.

Because you have no knowledge of Transatlantic slavery,
You cannot understand the horrors of the Middle Passage:
Kidnapped and commodified for the personal gains of others;
Sharks following the stench of slaves robbed of humanity.

Because you've never admired a fine head of Black hair,
"Yuh shave mi 'ead clean an' call me Cora Cunninghame,
Left me naked, bald 'eaded an' strip of everyt'ing;
Shipmates scatter far an' condemn to livin' death."

Because Merchant City was built with the blood of slaves,
You refused to count the cost of Scotland's imperial past.
The enslaved lay buried in no known grave in the bush:
Genteel widows, orphans living off the proceeds of sugar.

Because the inheritors introduced modern slavery legislation,
You tried to expunge memories of the house of bondage:
"I found Mrs Cobham in a terrible huff… She is much affected
By the fate of her Negro. But here comes the Coffee, farewell."[53]

'Janet Schaw's *Journal of a Lady of Quality*?
Marching into the seat of government in Edinburgh;
Walking through the corridors of Holyrood Palace.
'Reparations?' balked the Speaker: 'Move on, move on!'

---

53. See Janet Schaw's *Journal of a Lady of Quality* (New Haven, CT: Yale University Press, 1921), written between 1774 and 1776.

Ode to Joseph Knight and James Somerset

Walking the jaded streets of Merchant City
(With coat collar turned up against the howling wind),
Heading in a straight direction towards Trongate:
Knight standing in the midst of pride and prejudice!

Weaving in and out of city boundaries within boundaries,
Shape-shifting in the Cunninghame Mansion – GOMA[54] –
Listening to talk of black minstrelsy and musing:
Was it Knight who changed Alba's attitude to race?

Scotland, land of clans, where Knight was brought to toil
With his master, John Wedderburn of Ballindean:
Sugar baron whom Knight brought a freedom suit against;
Or was it James Somerset who inspired him to fight?

> Perhaps it was Lord Mansfield's ruling in England
> That turned the world of sugar upside down.

---

54. The Gallery of Modern Art (GOMA) Glasgow is a neo-classical palace that was built by a wealthy eighteenth-century tobacco lord named William Cunninghame.

Flinging Greek Fire at Meghan Markle

Let's scroll back three hundred years before
To Dido, "honorary white" niece of the great
Bewigged Lord Mansfield, he who outlawed
Slavery in England of the eighteenth century!

Dido, turbaned *"mulatto"* daughter of a Black
Enslaved woman whose self-assurance was
Caught on oil and canvas with Cousin Lizabeth,
Eligible belle wearing pearls with feather in cap.

Basking in the glory of her accomplishments as
Modern woman of colour (actress and blogger),
In walks Meghan Markle (daughter of dread-
Locked African-American) and bags HRH Harry.

Attacked by the media and labelled "uppity" for
Daring to get above herself (almost straight out
Of Compton), setting a global hare running on TV:
Loose Women, talk-shows, trolling and twittering!

That was the moment when Prince Charming
Knew he had to do something: the Firm, or the
Palace engine, issuing a stern rebuke against those
Royal ranters flinging Greek fire at Meghan Markle.

Remember Edward and Mrs Wallace Simpson?
A twice divorced American brought down the
British monarchy of Edward VIII. Aww! Charles
And Camilla outmanoeuvred Princess Diana.

Understandably, the pairing of MM and HRHH
Brought out the obnoxious side of muck rakers,
Digging up dirt on MM's slave heritage: "a low
Born," miscegenation and race degeneration.

Garnering considerable media focus, *paparazzi*
Stalking outside her home, lens zooming on her
Dog-haired riddled dark coat, yoga mat and the
His and Hers bracelet worn by MM and HRHH.

Much ado about would-be princess in waiting.
"Mi cyaan believe it!" Divorced thirty-something
International beige *Suits* actress and jetsetter
Waiting to marry into modern Royal menagerie.

Meghan Markle: a self-made millionaire!
Behind the façade of a humanitarian lay a savvy
Businesswoman with a tremendous amount of
Self-belief that she will enjoy a fairytale ending.

The View from Cardiff Castle: For Meghan Markle

Late afternoon, on a chilly Wednesday,
I found myself climbing the steep steps:
Up, up to the top of the keep at Cardiff
Castle with its ice-cold metal handrails.

"I'm on top of the world, ma!" An inner
Voice shouted, refusing to be silenced
By my reserved, cautious, sensible self
Who has come to Cardiff to represent…

"Pull up the drawbridge!" Did I imagine
Hearing male voices in suits of armour?
Echoes from another world: men ready
To defend the stronghold with their lives.

And there she was a day later: Meghan
Markle (escorted by her besotted prince),
Come to pay homage to a time long gone.
Princess to be but no damsel in distress.

Who would have thought that three years
Later she and her prince would be forced
To flee to the more tolerant City of Angels
And lend her voice to "Black Lives Matter"?

Who could have imagined she would
Have been driven out of this sceptred
Isle, this green and pleasant island, for
Daring to marry a drop of blue blood?

Fast forward to 2023: near catastrophic
Car chase (by *paparazzi*) in New York City!
Security removed from attractive targets:
"We upset the royal dynamic just by existing."

Whitewashing the Past

Flames of intolerance in the theatre of the oppressed:
Sores breaking out, hidden trauma in the body,
Songs spouting from "the souls of black folk,"[55]
Sorrow rolling like billows in their heads.

So many lives pulled up by root and branch,
Dispossessing Africa of its natural resources!
Ships ploughing through the trackless sea.
Enslaved actors playing their part in unchaining.

Compensation claims honoured by the Centre:
Sugar barons partaking of the banqueting dish;
Flexible jaws stretching to accommodate the feast!
Black stain on England's picture-perfect landscape.

> Whitewashing the past with history from above:
> Inheritors of blackness cauterising the wounds.

---

55. W.E.B. Du Bois, *The Souls of Black Folk* (Chicago: AC McClurg & Co, 1903).

Indelible Ink: The Triangular Trade

I have a rosewood writing desk with an inkwell,
And shelves stacked with books to tell.
You see my faced lined like the map of Fitzrovia,
But you cannot pin-point the town of Monrovia.

Because your hands are deep in Triangular trade,
You opened a deck of cards and called me spade.
Battling between hope and fear of a slave revolt,
You brought down the leader of the mob with a bolt.

Because I finally broke free of your chain-link,
You wrote me out of history with indelible ink.
And then, because you do not have the gift of speech,
You tried to silence me with your deafening screech.

> Much have I seen strapped to my foremother's back,
> But no matter how you try to break me, I won't crack.

Sonnet 18: Trade Winds

Shall I compare thee to the strong trade winds?[56]
Thou art more calm and gentler than the breeze,
Or the winds that carried African dust
Across the ocean to the West Indies.
Sometimes trade winds take different routes:
From the North East to a westerly path,
And also from the Southern Hemisphere –
By choice, strengthening in the winter months.
But thy calm summer breeze shall not change course,
Nor lose its gentleness across the miles;
Nor shall evening shadows draw nigh thee
When Father Time points a bony finger.

    So long as trade winds blow over the seas,
    So "long live sailing ships, commerce and thee."

---

56. Inspired by Jamaican poet David Neita's version of Shakespeare's "Sonnet 18."

Hurricane Dean (August 2007)

Two tropical trees came down in the storm:
One blocking the flow of rush hour traffic,
Wind swept branches with evergreen leaves;
Obstructing the path of man and machine.

Stout cedar lying lifeless and uprooted,
Earmarked for wood planks, floorboards and coffins.
Tough climbing vines clinging by their tendrils,
Trailing on cedar trunk like *coco-wis*.[57]

Tall Blue Mahoe trees standing on hillsides
With heart-shaped leaves wavering in the rain.
Bamboo trees forming a dense canopy
Of giant grasses buffering the gale force wind.

Fresh fruit piled high beside weedy stonewalls:
Seville oranges soured by nature's hand,
Thick fruited branches felled by natural forces,
Country cousins gathering up the spoils.

---

57. Vines growing on tree bark.

Unchaining the Imagination

Saturating young minds with messages,
Advertisers fuelling inferiority complex.
Negative images on television screens,
In magazines and retro comic books.

Stock images commanding youth's attention,
The clash of multi-cultures minimised by
Winning trophies outside the race:
Assimilation nullifying raised Black Power fist!

Negative phrases associated with skin type,
Traits, characteristics, commerce and trade:
Black widow, Black magic, Black Thursday!
Black Monday, Black hole, Black book, Black…

Peace-hating people and corrupt *politrickans*
Depending on aid and loans from the World Bank!
Fortress Europe trading with grown up partners:
Black skin white masks, mimic wo/men in suits.

Unchaining the imagination to think outside the box,
Salving wounds inflicted in Plantation America.
Self-affirmation and negation in the one breath,
Positive words woven and spoken each day.

Black backing singers surrounded by rock stars,
Hip-hop videos leaving little to the imagination,
Hiding kinky hair beneath wigs and weaves:
"And the coloured girls go: 'Doo do doo do…'"[58]

---

58. Lou Reed, "Walk on the Wild Side," https://www.youtube.com/watch?v=oG6fayQBm9w.

I Shall Return

In the dim and distant future, I shall return[59] again
On a burning day to see black backs bent
In fields of dreams deferred to a future date,
And to stalks of corn swaying in the breeze.

In the dim and distant future, I shall return again
(On a summer's day to harvest pimento berries),
To a time when man and plough merged as one,
And girls hid swollen stomachs in "the folly of youth."

In the dim and distant future, I shall return again
On a golden noon to visions of youth forgotten
(When dreams of freedom saddled the wind),
And silent rivers rushed to the fickle sea's embrace.

In the dim and distant future, I shall return again
(On a midsummer's night to feast on fried fish),
To a time when night wrapped itself around day,
And menopausal women longed for last blood.

In the dim and distant future, I shall return again
(On a breeze to watch the midnight sun go down),
To a time when old women wove Anancy stories,
Telling tales by the light of the wood fire.

In the dim and distant future, I shall return again
(On a stormy evening to hear the roll of thunder),
To a time when old men cried out to Shango,
And the moon looked down on the faces of the night.

---

59. Inspired by Claude McKay's renowned poem, "I Shall Return," https://poets.org/poem/i-shall-return.

Black Ivory: Call and Response

"*A chi-chi bud oh!*"[60] The call and response
Was kept up by the leader of the chain gang.
Sledge by sledge they laid into the rockstones,
Splitting boulders to build Empire road.

"*A chi-chi bud oh!*" Sparks flying, clouds fanning
Out across the evening sky but working day,
Far from over for sweating rough palm hands,
Swinging pick axes splitting rocks apart.

"*Som' a dem a 'oller...*" A few metres
In the gully old men caught the rhythm,
Rolling rocks for the sweating stone-breakers.
"Hu! Hu! *A chi-chi bud oh!* Hu! Hu!"

Entrusted with guiding the gang of men,
Building England's own Appian Way,
The leader covered each thud of the sledge
With a heavy grunt. "Hu! *Chi-chi bud oh!*"

"*Som' a lagga 'ead...*" Falling into line,
Hands swinging pick-axes and sledge hammers!
Beneath the dead leaves a galliwasp lurked,
Waiting to sink brittle teeth into black flesh.

"Whai-ee! *If you prick us do we not bleed?*"[61]
Galliwasp's sharp teeth punctured ashes skin.
"Hu! *A chi-chi bud oh!*" Black ivory
Grunting to each swing of the sledge. "Hu! Hu!"

"*Som' a white bud!*" A call to action
From a conch reverberating across the hills.
Chain gang toiling overtime without even
The King's shilling. "Hu! *Chi-chi bud oh!*"

---

60. Gloria Cameron, Sonia Singham and Yvonne Conolly, *Mango Spice: 44 Caribbean Songs* (London: A & C Black, London, 1988).
61. W. Shakespeare, *The Merchant of Venice*, Act III, Scene I.

The Stone-Breakers

"Day oh! Day a light an' me wahn go home!"[62]
A pageant of shapes passed through Time Tunnel,
Reminding to remember not to renounce,
Lest we forget the trauma of the land.

"Day oh!" Traditional plaid pink headties
Shrouding grey hair – textured like silk and steel.
Unsung s/heroes breaking stones with hammers
To erect parish boundaries and enclose common land.

"Day a light an'…" Expressions glazed over,
Hearing the call to action from the horn-man:
Ashanti warrior based in Trelawny,
Nursing his wrath in the Cockpit Country.

"Day oh!" Loose gravel falling from piles,
Heaped like pyramids in the Valley of Kings.
Buried deep in the rock a red ruby,
Lost by a Tartan *backra* back in the day.

"Day oh! Mi seh day, mi seh day, mi seh…"
A pageant of shapes passed through Time Tunnel,
Written out of the annals by Long and Edwards:
Work-worn hands turning the pages.

"Day oh!" Squatting on the site of pain,
Stone chips lodged in mucus eyes and sore feet,
Whitlow ravaging big toes and cracked fingers:
"Go dung a Manuel Road… Fi go bruk rock stone…"[63]

"Bruk dem one by one, gal an' bwoy…" The red
Stone seemed to pulsate like a heart beating:
A grim keepsake of the old Tam o' Shanter.
"Mash yuh 'an nuh cry, Matilda; for a play we a play…"

---

62. Cameron, Singham and Conolly (1988).
63. *Ibid.*

A Girl Writes Back: Ode to Rudyard Kipling

Someone I used to know once said, "The world
is a stage"[64] and each of us must take the exit
Down right, down left or use the back door,
Shuffling off: "*O sleep! O gentle sleep!*"[65]

That same someone, or perhaps another,
Once said, "If you can walk through minefields
And not get your feet blown off in the process,
The gods will assist those who stay the course."

If you can stand to sit on an aeroplane
For nine hours, flying cattle class to Jamaica,
And not visit Seville Great House plantation,
Where Spain fled the shores at Runaway Bay...

If you can stand on the Sukey River bridge
In James Hill and see a Claude McKay look-a-like,
Carrying a bundle of wood on his head,
And not recite: "So much have I forgotten..."[66]

If you can visit Marcus Garvey Archives,
And not think of this son of St Ann soil
Standing at Speaker's Corner, orating:
"Up, you mighty race, accomplish what you will..."

If you can visit the parish of St Thomas,
And not see Paul Bogle's statue in Morant Bay,
Or pause to remember George William Gordon,
And Queen Victoria's advice to the peasants...

If you can bear to see your birth place, St Ann,
Turned into an all-inclusive spot for tourists
(With our "bright stars" serving Planter's Punch),
And not stop the past from dictating your future...

---

64. W. Shakespeare, *As You Like It*, Act II, Scene VII.
65. W. Shakespeare, *Henry VI*, Part II, Act III, Scene I.
66. C. McKay, "Flame-Heart," https://www.poetry-archive.com/m/flame-heart.html.

If you can take a detour to "New York, New York,"
And visit the African Burial Ground Monument
Between Wall Street and the centre of trade,
And see idle black hands in downtown Brooklyn...

If you can plan to attend the Annual
Black Writers' Conference at Medgar Evers,
And watch *Ngugi wa Thiong'o* being honoured,
Or see Sonia Sanchez weeping for Treyvon Martin...

If you can visit the Schomburg in Harlem,
Touring the Research Centre for Black Culture,
Studying pictorial images of Obama's rise,
And not wish for a Black Prime Minister...

If you can take the High Road to Scotland,
Attending the Glasgow Commonwealth Games,
And not participate in the historical events,
Or fail to take a guided tour of Merchant City...

If you can stomach men in seats of learning
(Using colonial images to dictate our memories),
And not call for reparations from Britain,
Or take a walk down Jamaica Street, Glasgow...

If you can visit "the land of song" – Wales –
And not cite the Douglas-Pennants' slave past,
Or drop by Dylan Thomas' statute and recite:
"Do not go gentle into that good night..."[67]

If you can fly solo to Florida
(To attend a good old Jamaican Nine Night),
And face a bald-headed bigot on the flight,
Refusing to be bullied and harassed...

If you can sit in the Lyric Theatre in London
Watching imposters playing Michael Jackson,
Doing the Moon Walk or belting out "Thriller,"
And not object to the lack of pigmentation...

---

67. D. Thomas, "Do Not Go Gentle into That Good Night," https://poets.org/poem/do-not-go-gentle-good-night.

If you can take a no frills flight to Dublin
(Speak at an African/Caribbean diaspora event),
And endure the negation of Ireland's slave past:
Governor Sligo's Kelly's and Cocoa Walk estates!

If you can face a gun-toting cowboy neighbour
(Operation Trident jotting down suspiciously)
Without repeating aloud, "It is not for the
Brutalised to give comfort to the bystander..."[68]

If you can take a trip home in less than a year,
Bucking up faces at the annual church convention
(Names from the rain-lashed vales of childhood),
And finally close the door on that link to the past;

Then, Putus, yuh is a ooman, mi dawta,
An' tough enuff to walk dis far alone.

---

68. See Jessie W. Getting's BET acceptance speech, June 2016, https://www.youtube.com/ watch?v=B7VPMJcXPGs.

The Stranger in the Room

You, too, should have travelled,
Taken the road less trodden,
Walked with no means of transport,

Wandered along rural footpaths,
Visited places fallen into ruin,
Heard echoes of stifled voices from the past!

Do you suppose I care
Or that I've forgotten
How you tried to block my progress?

Can words really cut
Like a shard of broken crystal
Or a piece of cold sharp steel?

If memory serves me right,
You tried to dim my light,
Yet still I outshine you!

Do you suppose I fear
Coming to the podium late,
Being the stranger in the room?

Who said I couldn't succeed,
Couldn't shift the insurmountable
Obstacles in the way of my pursuit?

Though our paths cross occasionally,
Marking how far we've come,
Yet still I rise like an eagle.

Kool-Aid

I don't remember my mother's wet face:
The day she walked up the aeroplane steps,
Flying by BOAC to London
On a sunny afternoon with blue skies.

I don't remember when she went away:
The day I drank Kool-Aid to quench my thirst,
Watching sleek shiny fowls scratching around,
And roosters roughing up the scruffy hens.

I don't remember who picked me up then:
The day I fell off the wall in the yard, reciting,
"Solomon Grundy, Born on a Monday..."
Head hurting as if hit with a hammer.

Yet, in my mind's eye, I see her smiling,
Waving a white handkerchief back at me.

PART TWO
BRAATA

Meghangate

Voyage in the dark:
"Is there anybody there?"
None but the moon's glare.

Prince Harry's lament:
"Upside down they're turning me…"
Why can't you all see?'

"Straight out of Compton":
Commoner elbows English
Rose out of the way!

Meghangate affair:
"Oh, what tangled webs they weave,"
Trying hard to deceive.

Diana's car crash:
Vampires gorging on grief:
The old Fleet Street gang.

"What Meghan Wants"

Boy princes at war:
Men manipulated by
Agents of the crown.

An open sore that
Oozes blue blood at the mere
Sight of the press pack.

The "cheekie chappie"
That is doomed to remain a
Peter Pan at heart.

The talk of the town:
"What Meghan wants, Meghan gets."
Duke's "Duchess Diva."

Waiting to Exhale

Waiting to Exhale:
Meghan Markle in limbo,
Friends with daggers drawn.

Wisdom walks away.
Courage knows no bounds nor fear.
Dignity says "Go!"

A bit of singing
(Vincent painting his demons):
"Starry, Starry Night…"

The House of Windsor:
Erm, "Harry went to Hampstead.
Harry lost his hat…"

If they must make a
Mountain out of a molehill,
Why not scale the heights?

Scenes From Gatwick Airport

Scene 1: Customs Officer to Dread

"Anything to declare?"
The earth-man with waist-locks frowned.
"Yuh naah search mi dreads!"

"I'm taking the rum..."
"I gwine bruk up dem *plate-claat*!"[69]
Cho! Unu too tief."

"I need to frisk you."
"Get yer *pussy-claat* 'ands off me.
Dohn touch mi blood-seed!"

"Is that Rolex real?"
"Money on legs to *blow-wow*!"[70]
"Where is the receipt?"

Scene 2: Customs Officer to Elderly Lady

"That's a lot of food."
There were *stinking toes, bammies*...[71]
"Dohn squeeze-up mi tings."

"And what have we here?"
"Christmas cake fi mi *dawta*."
"A herb cake no doubt."

"That is a weapon."
"Is old-time clothes-iron, sah."
"Ah yes, the Antiques Road Show."

"Step this way, madam."
"Yuh tink mi nuh know mi rites?"
"You people are all..."

---

69. "A plate or dish cloth or tea towel": slang used instead of a swear word, much like "*pussy-claat*" or sanitary towel.
70. Similar to "wow."
71. "Stinking toe" is a fruit with a smelly seed pulp and is found in Jamaica and the Caribbean. The Latin name *hymenaea courbaril*. It is shaped like a toe. "Bammy/ies" is a thick flat bread made from cassava flour, usually eaten with fried fish.

Scene 3: Customs Officer to Young Woman

"How was the weather?"
"Weh dis *puss-yeye*[72] man a seh?
Yuh nuh see mi tan?"

"That's not hand luggage."
"Is mi granny grip…"
"It should have been tagged."

---

72. "Cat's eyes."

Guava Tree Over Cocoon Pond

Guavas on fruit tree
Bending over Cocoon Pond.
Fruit falling: "Plop, plop!"

Gaze on a Grecian Goddess

"Lawd, di statue stark…"
Fay undid her floral scarf.
"Cover 'er behind."

Scenes in Papine Market, Kingston (August 1999)

Miss Hetty in the Market:

"Yuh nuh know *braata*[73]?"
Miss Hetty was short of change.
"Wat! Yuh thief like pus!"

The Higgler to Miss Hetty:

"Mi nuh giv' *braata*."
She weighed a bunch of *guineps*.
"Gwan, gal. Yuh too cheap."

Miss Hetty to the Higgler:

"Time longer dan rope.
I gwine live fi see yuh cut
Dung to size, ole t'ief."

---

73. "A baker's dozen."

Celebrity Spotting at JFK Airport (June 2012)

"Oh my word! That's... No!"
They flew First Class to New York.
"Oh my word!" she screamed.

Victory in Sight: For HW Longfellow

The mounts by lofty women
Scaled and grasped were not
Reached by slow ascent.
But they, while their compatriots
Snoozed, were fighting battles
With victory in sight.

Mother and Child at Bus Stop

"Which city is the brightest in the world, Mum?"
The boy was scoffing a hot sausage roll.
Flaky pastry clung to his chubby cheeks.
"No, it's not Brighton. It's electricity."
He regurgitated at the crowded bus stop.
"Which city is called the Eternal City?
No, it's not heaven, Mum. It's Rome, silly."

Echoes

His lone voice echoes across the ocean,
Delivering the good news in stages,
Bringing bad tidings without emotion.
Often they sit in pews turning pages,
Trying hard not to show their rages,
Waiting patiently for others to offer,
Wondering: to proffer or not to proffer.

Blue Print: Upon a Father-in-Law's Death

He sat in his chair in former days,
Courting his sweetheart with the sunrays.
Nimble fingers threading needle in his head,
Hoping that they'd put on a proper spread.
Nurses drawing scarce supply of red blood,
Surprised to see it gushing out like a flood:
"I used to read blue print drawing at work."

Cocoa Basket: Upon a Grandmother's Death (July 2008)

Here she lies in state, as if in slumber,
Having given me her last cucumber.
Loose lips *labrishing*[74] over the casket,
Fretting who would get her cocoa basket.
Friends elated about seeing old mates;
Foes calculating the currency rates.

---

74. "Gossiping."

Dead Silence: Upon Losing a Child (December 1989)

He came into the world in dead silence,
Skin pale and colourless as cold liquid;
Not a sound, no gasping air for his brain.
White robes quietly examining the body.
Tears cascading down face, and broken heart;
Everyone talking about a fresh start.

Thread-Bag: Upon Losing a Great-Aunt to Dementia

"One hundred dozen eggs to the market!"
The old lady had boasted on camera.
Neglected by her kin and hard of hearing,
The storyteller and Sunday School teacher:
Guardian of our family's memory.
She stood by her door in rags and broken shoes,
Staring into the camera: "I was a *higgler*."

The Drowning: Green Grotto Cave

Blind fish swam in the lake in the grotto,
A tourist attraction on the North Coast.
It was here that runaways hid in flight,
Pulling foot from the plantation system.
Confused ratbats haloed the mother's head:
"Plop!" The child slipped under the coal-black water.

Grumpy Old Man

Not many things enraptured the old man
Except observing the constellations,
Watching out for his grey homing pigeons,
And seeing *chic* ladies in seamed stockings.
He loathed his wife's blue rinses, Sunday shopping,
Young people wearing headphones in public,
And "gals" with slippers hanging off their toes.

Swan Lake Neck

Many things boiled up in the lord of the dance:
He disliked short stubby toes and cracked heels,
Bony knees, big bottoms and thick calves!
Aww! He loved seeing rainbows[75] in the sky!
A *danseur*, he liked a clean pair of ankles,
A slender waist show-cased in leotards,
And he loved a long graceful Swan Lake Neck.

---

75. This collection was completed on Saturday 2 March 2024 at 15.30 when a rainbow arched my bedroom window! Prior to the rainbow's appearance, the doorbell rang several times, but there was no one there. I knew then that *Walk-Foot Woman*, which I began in 2007, was finally finished.

POSTSCRIPT: REFLECTIONS ON WALK-FOOT WOMAN AND OTHER POEMS

When I was asked to endorse this wonderful collection of poetry, little did I know that the poet, Dr. Velma McClymont, would be taking me on a sentimental journey into the hills of rural St Ann, Jamaica, and into the hinterland. Reading many of the poems in the collection, I was struck by the descriptions of a time and place that has passed into history. After an initial first reading, I could not help reading aloud and airing my thoughts: "What a collection of inspirational and reflective verses! Hilarious and serious, the famous and infamous. Indeed, this gem from Jamaica should be available in schools, colleges, libraries and archives across the island."

Rather than offering an in-depth analysis of the collection, I have selected some of the more memorable poems, and have given an overview of each one. As a starting point for a discussion about the themes prevalent in Caribbean and Black British poetry, the poems selected also demonstrate the intertextual nature of the works produced by writers who were exposed to the colonial education system in the Caribbean during the twentieth century, and prior to the post-Independence period.

"Walk-Foot Woman" is an aptly chosen title that reflects the cultural expression of a rural female who does not own the luxury of a motorcar. This was especially the case during the colonial period when rural women (*higglers*) walked for miles to adjacent hill villages, to St Ann's Bay Market or Kellits Market in the parish of Clarendon to sell their farm produces.

"Pilgrim Stick" is reminiscent of the title of John Bunyan's allegorical book, *The Pilgrim's Progress*. In this narrative poem, the poet makes use of religious symbolism and metaphors to drive her message home: thus, compelling the reader to think of creation and one's origin.

"The Mad Doctor of Edinburgh Castle" (a real castle that was built in the hills of St Ann by a Scottish man during the eighteenth century) is a historical narrative poem that speaks about the importance of preserving stories about slavery, even of an infamous murderer such as Lewis Hutchinson.

Anyone with any knowledge of the Land of Wood and Water cannot help but experience nostalgia from reading about the birds and fruit portrayed by their exotic and local names in "The Island of Springs: Ode to the West Wind". What is more, the poem's title conveys notions of the English education that was transported to the British colonies. "Ode to the West Wind" is a poem written by Percy Bysshe Shelley in 1819. But it is "The West Wind" by the English poet and writer John Masefield that is remembered in "The Island of Springs," which shows the Jamaican-born poet's "longing for home."

"Drumilly Remembered" is another nostalgic poem in which the poet appeals to the senses. Here readers are transported into the setting of this rural village that is hidden far off the beaten track.

In "A Better Future: Ode to Langston Hughes," the poet acknowledges Hughes' poem, "A Dream Deferred", as a source of inspiration, and equally rails against systemic racism in the British education system, asking,

> What happens to high ambition delayed?
> Does it burn bright like a light in the dark,
> Does it loiter on the streets of destiny
> Or does it fight for a better future?

"If We Must Live" is a much-loved poem by the Jamaican-born poet and writer Claude McKay, whom Dr. McClymont proudly acknowledged as her muse in her historical novel, *Little River*. With his "fierce hatred of injustice," McKay is an inspiration to many writers and activists in the Caribbean Diaspora in the UK and USA.

In "The Ivory Tower: Ode to the White House," again McClymont pays homage to her muse, McKay. Pointing a finger at the education system that has placed barriers in the way of many Black academics, the speaker in this poem maintains her dignity whilst walking past this symbol of white privilege that limits and thus deskills Black excellence.

"Insurmountable Heights: Ode to Marcus Garvey" is a truly fitting tribute to Jamaica's national hero, the Hon. Marcus Garvey, who fought against racial injustice in America and rallied the descendants of enslaved Africans under the banner of "Black consciousness." In this poem, McClymont compels her readers to find and rediscover their heroes from places such as Jamaica and the wider Caribbean.

In "The Shadow: Ode to Walter de la Mare," looking back to schooldays, de la Mare's sonnet "Silver" was a favourite poem.

However, it is de la Mare's other poem, "The Listeners," about a traveller knocking "on a moonlit door", that is the inspiration for "The Shadow." In this poem, the poet uses nature and sounds to cast a poetic spell on her readers. Note the effective use of onomatopoeia, which appeals to other senses.

Throughout the collection, there is a sense of place, displacement and a focus on the exotic Other. "Eight Rivers" draws us into the Jamaican landscape and proceeds to manipulate our senses:

> The night jasmine wafts her scent
> On the tropical breeze,
> While sturdy South Sea roses sprout
> In an invisible realm of fragrance and odours.

"Footprints Upon Our Souls" is a melancholy poem that reminds me of a song by Ray Williams, titled "Growing Old" (I'll Never Grow Old). In this poem, celebrating the Windrush generation, the focus is on the passage of time, the aging process and the impact of migration. Here, the poet urges readers to be selective of good memories, and to shed those that hurt us. "Fossils in Rocks" should be read alongside "Footprints." This particular poem acts like a balm, offering healing to the readers of the trauma experienced on the journey from the Caribbean to Britain during the Windrush era. In this sonnet, the last stanza offers advice and healing: "The things we forget should remain dormant/Like buried treasure or fossils in rocks."

In "David Livingstone's Promised Land," the focus shifts from Britain to Africa, which was described by the early European writers as a land with no history, culture or religion. Thus, during the so-called "civilising mission," British missionaries such as David Livingstone and others were seen as torch bearers. Africa, meantime, was regarded as "the dark continent," evil and backward. Note the poet's use irony in stanza 3:

> Africa, they said, was beguilingly seductive!
> Darkest Africa, Livingstone's promised land:
> "His body was hung over a tree to dry,
> Embalmed and shipped back to England."

Military history is a subject that raises its head often because of its erasure (whitewashing of the past) of the contributions of Caribbean service personnel who fought in the two world wars in Europe: 1914–1918, and 1939–1945. This is evident in poems such as "Barbed Wire on the Western Front", and "The Call to Action." McClymont seems not to be enamoured by the enlisting of men from the Caribbean, who were enticed ("Your King and country need you"), and encouraged to fight for the Mother Country that discriminated against them during the war and after. Even as "Afrikan Remembrance Day" pays tribute to our unknown fallen soldiers in World War I, the poet offers a scathing criticism of England's use of Black men who were not honoured after the Great War:

> Commonwealth wreath-laying at the Cenotaph,
> Celebrating our heroes with hymns and harps,
> Recalling their contributions to the Great War,
> Making the ultimate sacrifice for their King...

While the three poems above explore the British West Indies Regiment's contribution to World War I, "Mutiny in Taranto: Ode to Mr. James Fairweather" is concerned with World War II. In this poem, the pains of the wounded, and families of the West Indies regiment, are preserved by the old soldier, who is reflecting on the past:

> "Some of mi comrades sleeping in eternal darkness."
> There was an urgency to put his story on paper.
> "Colonel Lipton was my MP in Lambeth in di '50s...
> Nurse, turn up di TV – time fi East Enders."

"Ration Books in Battersea" is another narrative poem that speaks directly to the Windrush pioneers who came to London and settled in Battersea (in the borough of Wandsworth) directly after World War II. The contrast between the post-war years and wartime is explored here. There is a sense of nostalgia for bygone days:

> It wasn't like this in my day, the war years:
> Hands springing up like mushrooms in schoolrooms,
> Bombed and evacuated to the Kent countryside;
> Pink cheeked lasses hop-picking in cotton smocks.

"No Coloureds, No Irish, No Dogs" is a telling poem that records the cold reception received by the migrants from the then British West Indies during the post-war era. The hopes and dreams of migration for a better life are shattered by the lived reality of the Caribbean immigrants, as reflected in the poem's title.

> Anticipation built up on the sea voyage,
> But the cold heart of the city greeted them!
> Front doors slamming in weary dark faces:
> "*Sorry, no coloureds, no Irish, no dogs.*"

In "Fire Sparkle," the poetic voice returns to the Caribbean landscape where the speaker seeks refuge from the cold welcome received in London, as noted in "No Coloureds, No Irish, No Dogs" and "Ration Books in Battersea." Childhood memories are etched indelibly on the mind. Given McClymont's love of the Jamaican rural landscape, it is not surprising that the poet takes a journey down memory lane, dreaming and weaving memories of schooldays and the marketplace in this poem.

Finally, "Yabba Pot: The Good old Days" demands to be read aloud, preferably as a performance piece. In this long narrative poem, the poet puts all the ingredients into one large cast iron pot, evoking a sense of nostalgia for childhood, those early years imprinted in her memory. On this journey to becoming, the poet takes her readers back to her rural beginning where the speaker asks:

> What happened to the days when our women
> Carried grip baskets at their sides in the hills
> Where farmers planted *Gros Michel* bananas,
> And gave each other a day's work in lieu?

In those nostalgic lines, I myself was transported back to a time when women in rural Jamaica carried grips and baskets "at their sides in the hills", and *Gros Michel* bananas were plentiful. I can almost hear the poet reciting "Yabba Pot." Indeed, *Walk-Foot Woman and Other Poems* is a must-read book.

Rev. Delroy Sittol JP,
Jamaica Baptist Union.

ACKNOWLEDGEMENTS

This collection would not be complete without acknowledging a number of people who believed in me, especially my dear grandmother, Mrs Carmel Smith-Morris, for whom I wrote "Cocoa Basket: Upon a Grandmother's Death" and "The Stone-Breakers", and my great-aunt, Mrs Vandalyn Smith-Grant, who was a wonderful storyteller. "Thread-Bag: Upon Losing a Great-Aunt to Dementia" is a tribute to her. "Blue Print: Upon a Father-in-Law's Death" acknowledges my late father-in-law, Mr David McClymont.

I would be remiss if I did not mention my late parents, who were part of the Windrush generation and who faced anti-black racism in 1960s London. "No Coloureds, No Irish, No Dogs" and "Ration Books in Battersea" are dedicated to my mother. My father loved American Westerns and boxing, especially featuring Muhammed Ali. Needless to say, "The Way West" and "The Kentuckian King of Boxing" were inspired by him.

I extend gratitude to my husband, Henry, and my adult children, Gavin and Rebecca. They have been on my literary journey since the 1990s, and have spent years listening to me reading and performing my work (poetry and prose) privately and publicly.

I thank Rev. Delroy Sittol (Jamaica Baptist Union, Jamaica) for endorsing this collection. I am eternally grateful to my muse, Claude McKay, whose poems have carried me through good times and bad. Indeed, "Brooklyn Heights" is a tribute to him and also "I Shall Return." As a child, going to school in the hills of rural Jamaica, I loved reciting poetry, especially McKay's poems: "The Spanish Needle" and "Flame-Heart."

I am grateful to my mentor, Jamaican-born scientist and anti-racist activist Professor Sir Geoff Palmer OBE, who resides in Scotland and has spent many years researching Scotland's role in the Transatlantic slave trade. "Ode to Joseph Knight and James Somerset" and "David Livingstone's Promised Land" are dedicated to him. He kindly agreed to write the foreword for *Walk-Foot Woman and Other Poems*.

Finally, I would like to thank Dr Nicola Frith for her editorial support and for writing the introduction to this collection.

ABOUT THE AUTHOR

Born in St Ann, Jamaica, Dr. Velma McClymont is a writer, poet, scholar-activist, creative writing tutor and the publishing director of WomanzVue. She has performed her poetry/spoken in Scotland (Glasgow; Edinburgh), England, Wales (Cardiff), Austria (Vienna), the USA (Florida; NY) and also in Jamaica (where she has worked as a visiting author and motivational speaker in schools, libraries and in faith settings).

In October 2022, McClymont published her fifth book, a historical novel titled Little River. A proud Jamaican-born British woman writer, her novel has been praised by the African Caribbean Institute of Jamaica/the Jamaica Memory Bank: "This piece of work is indeed seminal as it offers fresh insight into the relations between enslaved Africans in Jamaica and their Scottish colonisers within the context of plantation life."

A prolific writer of poetry and prose, Walk-Foot Woman and Other Poems is McClymont's sixth book. Also known as author Kate Elizabeth Ernest, under her pseudonym, she has written four books for children (see Other Books by the Author). Her seventh book is a children's picture book titled A Home for Mr. No-Roach, which is due to be published in June 2024.